A Riddle Without Any Answer...

At last, the king stood up and clapped his hands together mightily.

"I would like to welcome a guest tonight, the master storyteller Garim!"

A hooded figure at the far end of the table got up slowly and put back his hood. He made his way to a chair beside the massive fireplace. Now he threw his arms out beside him, and spoke in a commanding voice.

"I am the simplest of all things, so that even a child can find me. Many know my name but never find me, while others find me without knowing what they found. I can be found anywhere by anyone, but no one can see me, no matter where they look..."

Wendell did not know the answer. But as the storyteller spoke he felt his heart burning at the sound of the words, as if he had known the answer all his life and had just remembered it...

Wendell and the Dragon's Heart

Michael Rains

ISBN 978-0-578-02769-2

Published by Michael Rains

Cover Art by Lien Phan and Michael Rains

With thanks to Christine, Brianna, Joy, and John for always pestering me to write the next chapter.

Prologue : The Tale of Curdie

Once there was a very ordinary boy named Curdie. He was not strange or magical or peculiar, and if you saw him you probably would not notice him. He was an orphan, and wandered the streets of the royal city with the dogs and rats.

No one knew who he was, but still he was good and true at heart, and kept after himself and the other street urchins, but never by way of stealing or harm. They all looked up to Curdie, even the ones who were older than him.

One day there was a clamor in the square, and Curdie hurried to look. All were gathering around a man in fine clothes with his servants blowing great trumpets.

The great blasts carried all the way into the peasant's fields. Curdie watched from the edge of the crowd eagerly, and climbed a miller's wagon to see.

The servant took out a long, embellished scroll. Holding it high, he read in a very loud voice:

"Hear ye, hear ye, all citizens of this fair city of King Amondras, be it known in his 32nd year, there is hereby proclaimed great rewards to anyone who can rid the caves of Bardur from the ogre which has come to dwell therein, wreaking harm on travelers who would pass by and seizing their lawful goods. The reward shall be:"

He paused and looked.

"Ten thousand sacks of gold, a mirror of purest silver, and one wish to be granted of the king himself, be it great or small. And the king's own daughter shall marry them."

The man rolled up the scroll and mounted quickly on his horse, and in a swift moment was gone, the two trumpeters following. Now Curdie was always brave and clever. He borrowed a candle from the good miller who was always kind to him. He went down to the stream and gathered a sack of shiny stones, and kept these around his belt even though it was no more than a rope.

On his way through the square at night, he happened on soldiers from the castle sitting and laughing. When they saw him, they left from their drinking and asked him, "Where does such a tattered lad as thee go on a night such as this?"

Curdie pulled himself up bravely, though he was not much higher than their sword hilts, and told his plan to dispel the ravenous ogre. At this the men laughed heartily and threw him a gold coin.

Now the entrance to the cave was past a place where the reedy rushes blow in the wind, and through the swamp where the bubbles burble, and into the place where the rocks drip. Curdie lit his candle with a flint and proceeded into the murky cave, dropping a shiny stone every fifth step. When he had explored a bit this way, he retreated, following the shine of the stones in the candlelight. And so he continued the next night, and the next, each time bringing more stones.

Now it happened that the soldiers who had laughed at him were sitting guard outside the princess's room, where she was combing her hair. And by chance she heard them laugh about the boy who went to fight the ogre. Hearing them laugh more and more, she became more and more curious about who it could possibly be.

At last she opened the door and asked to be taken to him, but they would not that she should. At last they gave in to her entreaties, and told her of how he passed by the square at a certain hour every night.

But on the way out the king detained them, wondering how it was that she should go. She replied, "If I am to be given in marriage to whoever should accomplish this your task, is it not right that I should at least accompany them on their journey to give them help and strength?"

And the king, being wise at heart, finally relented.

So the princess and the two guardsmen met Curdie along the square and asked if they might accompany him on his journey, and he agreed. Now firstly, they passed by the place where the reedy rushes blow in the wind, and the princess said, it is the ogre! He is breathing. But Curdie said, no, it is the rushes, they do bend every night these past nights.

And then they went through the swamp, where the bubbles come up, and the first guardsmen said, hark, the ogre's stomach, he is hungry. But Curdie said, no, it is the bubbles burbling, as they do every night these past nights. And then they entered the cave where the rocks drip, and the second guardsman said, it is the ogre's feet, he is walking after us. But Curdie said no, it is the rocks dripping, as they do every night these past nights.

And Curdie led them along the long path, twisting and bending through the dark caves, until he came to the end of his stones. And then there was a sound of laughing. And the princess said, is it the laughing that is every night these past nights? And Curdie said, no, it is the ogre, he is laughing at us. Look!

And the guards shone their torches ahead, and there was the ogre, chuckling with his great belly.

And he said to them, "Are you not lost travelers? I will not that you should pass unless you have given me a hundred pieces of gold, else I will eat you. "

And his hideous face did roil with laughter. At this the two men did cower back, but Curdie bravely stepped ahead, and the princess followed right behind him.

Now the ogre was so used to having people be terrified of him and run away, that when Curdie came stepping towards him with no sign of fear, he began to wonder if this common boy had some great strength that made him invincible. And since all wickedness is cowardly, the ogre began to fear in his heart and trembled. But Curdie just shook his finger at the ogre and spoke plainly to him –

"You big, mean beast! Don't you know you shouldn't frighten the travelers and take their goods. "

The ogre was ashamed, because he was not very smart and no one had ever bothered to tell him that he should not frighten people. And he began to cry, his great sobs spilling big ogre tears onto the ground.

"Stop your blubbing!" Curdie said, "now, you must give back everything you took. And you must stop scaring the travelers."

And so in the end, the ogre became a help to the people of the city, and the princess married Curdie willingly, for she had seen that he was brave and true. And as they passed through the streets of the city in a celebrating procession, the air was filled with the people's cheering and brightly colored things.

1

The storyteller looked down from the night stars and let his eyes rest on the folk who huddled around his fire.

Children looked on without seeing, their eyes wide with memories of colored things and laughter and cheering that seemed to lilt in the air even now. No one said anything for a long time, and at last there was nothing left of the story but the cold night air and the steady crackling of the great fire. The storyteller looked around at the villagers, his eyes steady and bright.

"That is the beginning of the tales of Curdie, the orphan," he said seriously.

One by one, the people began getting up. Someone went up and put out a strong hand of gratitude.

"You've certainly earned your roast pig, old man," he said, as the storyteller shook his hand steadily.

One boy watched from a far edge of the fire pit, his eyes serious and watchful. One by one the people left, giving the storyteller coins and trinkets and compliments. At last no one was left but the boy. The storyteller gathered his sack and turned to go. The boy walked up beside him, and the old man looked down at the young face.

"Are those stories really true?" he asked, his small voice whispering earnestly. The storyteller turned and bent down to answer him, the edge of his mouth whisking into an amused grin. For a moment he said nothing. Then he spoke.

"Are they true, you say? Well now, do you think they are true?"

The boy looked down and turned his mouth into a line. He piped up.

"Well, how could they be true? I have never seen anything really that was like it was in your stories."

The old man knelt down by the boy, a wry smile still in the corner of his mouth.

"Well, your mother will be waiting for you. Why don't we talk about this tomorrow?"

The child stared at him, as if watching clouds.

"I have no mother," he said plainly, like reciting a laundry list. The old man picked up a rock and looked down at it, rolling it in his fingers.

"Oh… oh… I see." he said, speaking in a hushed tone. "Well, in that case, why don't we talk now."

He said no more and continued walking along, and the boy rambled along beside him, going ahead and then back, as if impatient. The old man turned and walked steadily up a slope, and the boy clambered up ahead, the bushes and trees on either side like a great black emptiness swirling in the freezing wind.

After a while they reached a small flat space, free of rocks and brush. As the boy climbed up, he saw the whole town spread out ahead of him like a huge lumpy blanket below the hilltop, twinkling with a few lights. The air was clear and fresh here, and filled with the scent of wild forest heather.

The old man made his way up behind him, and at last came up beside the boy in the center of the clearing, straightening up and looking a bit stronger than before, looking about and putting his hand to his belt. The boy gazed down at the town, watching all the great lumps of buildings as they slept in the wide darkness of the land.

The man pointed up into the sky now, and for the first time the boy looked up, up, into a vast swirling of night stars. As he looked at them, he felt that nothing had ever existed before these stars before, that he had been gazing at all the endless lights forever, as they formed pictures too beautiful to have any end, that spread out with no beginning or ending, one into the other. The old man stood beside him and watched as well, patient and still. Finally he spoke.

"Are the stories real… now that, is a fine question. Few ask it anymore, and even fewer care. Most think that I tell stories for a glass of ale or a piece of bread, and are content simply to laugh for the night and bask in the warmth of the story and the fire, listening as one listens to a meaningless song."

"Some of them were true once, but that was so long ago that they are now very different than when they happened. Some are made up entirely. But some, I believe, are truly real, however fantastic they may be. Heroes of long ago… who by some hidden way, discovered their destinies and made us remember the way things were made to be…"

"Life can sometimes seem like a broken story… wandering, pointless, and without end. So much so that we almost forget it was a true story to begin with - that there was ever anything good in it. But if we will believe our life is still a good story, and act like we would if our story was still whole - not becoming part of the twisted brokenness of it – then, I believe we will see things like in these stories I have told, so often that they are like my old friends, like the cloak I wear."

He lowered his voice to a whisper and bent down beside the boy.

"That… is the meaning of these stories. But you must keep this truth in your heart, and never let it go, never!"

The old storyteller stood up straight again and looked up at the stars, his hands on his belt, his voice trailing on as if it were indeed flying up to them…

"Some men live their whole lives and leave nothing behind them but dust, added to the dust of those who came before."

2

The windmill squeaked and squawked in the wind and the grinding of the millstone went on. Sunlight was bright on the ground outside the wagon, and lit on the edges of the straw like pure golden fire.

Wendahl sat up, as much as he could under the wagon, and stared for a while. Nothing went past. Then he crawled out quickly from under and went along down the scraggly dirt road.

The well water felt cold and sharp in the stranger's bucket. The water rippled to stillness after a moment. A boy stared up at him from the bottom, ringed with the perfect blue sky. He was too old to be "just a boy" and much too young to be "a man".

Dark chestnut locks fell on his face. The face looked out from the water every day. Once it had been so small. Today it was not, but the passage of time was so slow. Wendahl did not remember when it had grown.

A thousand smells and sounds of the market greeted Wendahl as he huddled against the sharp morning wind. He always liked the marketplace in the morning; it was like all the great confusion swallowed him until he was just another part of the clamorous music. Squeaks of wheels and spinning wheels and waterwheels, filthy boots stomping past, lumpy rolls, the last winter apple, a fresh scent of hay, the stench of the meatman's bloody sides.

No one seemed to notice the short boy who dawdled around the baker's awning, hopping on one foot and fiddling his fingers behind his back.

Now he turned and leaned on the table, looking around, watching a bird that hopped on the roof, or the other children playing and squealing by the horse's water. He hopped up now, and listened.

"Coming mother!" he yelled obediently, and ran off quickly, ducking between the people walking by. The baker looked up for a moment and smiled a little.

He ran across the way between two low houses and kept going, one way and another. Now there were fewer people and he slowed and walked down a desolate street, a bit dusty and with bits of straw strewn about.

Two other boys lingered around, walking aimlessly. The first one, Colin, was a bit taller and thin, with a moppish head and a sad, bored expression, as if he had watched the butcher cut up lambs all morning, and the other, Derrick, was just an ordinary type, with brown hair and a typical boyish look.

"Hallo Wendahl," the moppish one said, not unkindly. "Have you got anything yet?"

Wendahl reached inside his shirt calmly and pulled out a few puffy looking bread rolls.

"You're the best, Wendahl, the best, you know?" Derrick said appreciatively, and he handed them each a roll. Then began what looked like a solemn ceremony. They sat down in a ring, and began leisurely tearing off pieces and stuffing them in their gaping mouths.

After a while Derrick piped up, his mouth still gnawing on a big piece.

"You know, if I was as good as you at stealin', Wendahl, I bet I would've stole all the gold in the castle by now. I tried my hand at stealing rolls once, but the baker he caught me by the wrist real quick, and they threw me in the dungeon for a good while. It was real nasty in there, lots of rats and such, but not that different than living down by the peasant's land. Of course, everyone's tried to steal rolls before. Easy and quick. But there's no one like you, Wendahl, no one."

And with that he started on a long chuckle, rocking a little with it, the roll still in his mouth.

Colin, the sad boy, looked up, his eyes moving about slowly and watchfully. He had long, yellow hair that drooped over his head like wet straw.

"I tried to get a roll once," he said simply. "They just sent me to a lady out by old man Cralth's field, who put me to work on potatoes and weevils. It was real hard work, and she beat me sometimes, but once in a while I could get a potato."

He said nothing more.

They continued their solemn eating in silence, until only the sad boy was left with some. They got up, and kind of dusted themselves off really quickly, although it didn't do much. Derrick kicked a straw with his foot.

"What do you want to do today?" he said. "I've been hanging around the blacksmith's, hoping to get some work, fetching coal or something," he continued.

He looked off to the side into the distance, then looked down at his raised foot. Wendahl spoke up.

"Let's go to the Black Mongrel. Maybe we can find another drunk and get a few coins off the floor."

With mute agreement, they wandered along up the narrow side street.

It was a bit loud in the Black Mongrel, and the air smelled of things that were unpleasant at the beginning but had since had lots of time to grow even more unpleasant. It was dark inside, and a few torches gave a kind of grudging light to the black pitched walls. There were tables of rough wood, and a servingman in a greasy apron stood behind the counter. The two other boys wandered aimlessly by the benches, looking down at their feet.

"Hey, boy!" a rasping voice called out.

Wendahl turned, and looked over at the front, where an old man sat perched on a bench like a withered hawk. He had an eye patch, and when he saw the boy his face broke into a wide grin, the smile pushing through innumerable wrinkles of time, like the splintering of an old tree. He gave an uncouth laugh, and patted Wendahl on the head.

"So you're still alive, boy? You're growing strong, I see, just like I was once."

And he gave a horrible cough.

"And how are you, Nate, you old badger?" Wendahl said without politeness or malice.

"Not as well as I used to be," he replied with a bit of seriousness. "That's why I wanted to see you."

He patted a short sword hanging on his belt, really more of a dagger.

"I can't handle this very well anymore. I'm getting old, very old, and I wanted to make sure it went to someone deserving of it."

He gave a rumpled chuckle of amusement.

"I still remember that day when Billy Oakens pushed you down," he said proudly. "So I've decided to give it to you when you turn fifteen."

Then his voice turned grim and sober again.

"Anything younger than fifteen is too young to have a sword. You'll have to prove to me that you can learn to use it properly, boy, before I'll give it to you."

Wendahl grinned and gave a short laugh. He spit in his hand and stuck it out. The old man did the same, and they gave a short shake. Then the old man reached in a dirty pouch and pulled out a brassy looking coin. He pressed it in the boy's hand.

"Go get yourself a melon without thieving it for once, and leave an old man to his drink."

With that he laughed like an old crow and took a swig from his tankard.

Wendahl turned and went to look for the others. The people in the tavern sat at the tables, some drinking or laughing or singing. He soon saw them at the back, and went over to them.

"I got a copper," Colin said resignedly.

Derrick shrugged and said nothing.

"I got a brassy from Nate," Wendahl said.

They stood around a bit, looking across the tables, then one by one began going to the door. A taller, older looking boy stood by the entrance, his face bloated with a sour expression, chawing on a piece of wheat.

"Still scrounging for coppers in the vomit, Colin?" he spat out, and the sad boy just drooped along. Wendahl went past, and briefly looked up at the older boy. They stared for a moment but said nothing, and then all three went out.

"I'm not afraid of you!" the older boy called out from the doorway behind them.

The dust in the street had been thicker than the heat from the sun on that day, long before. Wendahl remembered it, how hot the dirt was, not only on the ground, but in the air and in his eyes. The memory itself was a picture scratched in the hot earth somewhere in his mind, baking with the fumes of the day. He didn't remember exactly how it started, or why.

Billy stared at him from across the street. His face was puffed dangerously, his clothes were torn in places and stained. Two years older than Wendahl, he was already big for his age.

"You've got something you stole from the market. I know. I've seen you."

He walked on, ignoring him. Billy walked along quickly after him.

"Give me some and I won't tell," he said teasingly. "Just a bit. Ay, I'm talking to you, you little whit."

A few other children gathered around.

"I know you think you're so great, Wendy, just because you can pinch a few rolls from the dumb baker. He's so stupid, anyone could do it."

"So, why don't you?" Wendahl asked plainly.

The boy wheedled, "Because I'm not a thieving bastard like you. Hey, come here!"

He pulled on the back of Wendahl's shirt, wheeling him around. Other children came and formed a ring around them, watching curiously, some shouting. Wendahl stood at one side, his face red and serious. It seemed as if time had stopped, and he had been standing there a long time, with the children always shouting and watching and the dust everywhere and the older boy staring down at him with his big, angry face.

"I'm not a bastard," he murmured quietly. "I had a father once," he continued, a mite louder, stepping ahead.

The other boy reached out with one hand and pushed him a little. He fell back into the dirt with a crash, and suddenly it seemed like something was roaring inside him, a roaring that seemed to drown out everything else. The other children yelled and shouted directions and stamped all around, like the inside of a whirling thunderstorm, and suddenly he got up and ran at the older youth.

He remembered that he got hit, and hard, but he hit back, again and again, until at last he stood heaving and trembling, looking down at the unconscious form of the larger boy, his fingers digging into his hands, his breath coming in great gasps. Colin, his sad face bewildered, came over and looked at him. Others came over as well, their faces fearful and serious. Wendahl looked back at them, not able to say anything.

"Are you okay?" he heard Colin ask suddenly.

The memory of that distant day shattered, and Wendahl snapped his head up quickly.

"Yeah…" he said, and shrugged.

They continued down the street away from the Black Mongrel.

3

There were great throngs in the village square, sitting and standing in the firelight. Their different colored garments were drab but had an air of festiveness. Wendahl stood at the side of an old, old tree, leaning and shivering.

"The people are rather generous with their vittles tonight," he said.

Derrick tossed a rock between his hands. Colin sat on the ground in a heap, motionless.

"I could share some right now," Colin observed plainly.

Derrick spoke up.

"We could get some I bet, right Wendahl? Come on! What's your plan?" he cajoled.

Wendahl looked over a bit, and seemed to stop shivering for a moment. He spoke calmly.

"Well, there's about five families sharing that pig over by the stone. I figure we could always belong to a different family than the one we're nearest too. If you don't look out of sorts who's going to ask?"

The other boy, Derrick, smiled a wide, wide grin.

"Don't get too cocky, if your plans always worked we could of had a roast chicken by now of our own."

Wendahl looked up.

"No, no… no, no… if Colin hadn't tripped we would've gotten past the kitchen door easy, and the woods are right by Cralth's fields."

"Yeah, that and that crazy fat woman. I've never had to duck a broomstick like that before, not even while living with my step Grandmother! Are you okay, Colin? Heh heh, I swear she was going to beat you bloody. You've got to learn how to scurry, Colin, not just sit there like a dope while they swat at you."

The two of them laughed, and Colin kind of guffled happily a bit. Wendahl looked for a moment, paying attention, and kind of moseyed along out from under the tree. The other two followed behind, walking with no hurry and seemingly without aim.

They reached a group of people, and walked along nicely. Wendahl went up to a table, decked out with a succulent roast pig and some bowls of earthy looking vegetables and sauces. He grabbed a bone, and took a big bite, leaning on the table. His two companions smiled back at him.

There was a commotion at the center of the square, people giving a loud cheer and hurrahing, and everyone seemed to quiet down. Then the strumming of an instrument was faintly heard, and slowly grew louder. A brisk tenor's voice licked syllables out of the air, which seemed to fly to Wendahl's ears over the distance. The roast pig was full of fatty juices, which began to fill up all the cold air in him and warm the whole world.

He felt the excitement of the families around him and the music danced up into the sky, and it seemed that there had always been laughter and music in the square, that it had never been an ordinary place where villagers simply passed through.

The minstrel played many songs, some which people would clap and skip to and some that they would just sit and listen to, still as the sky.

Soon he forgot about the roast pig and the cobblestones and the chill breeze that would blow every now and then, and only knew of old tales of love and woe, of dismal dungeons where lost lovers waited forever, of monstrous creatures from ever below, of blade and fire and beauty and spire, of towers that climbed higher and higher, of secrets untold, mysteries of old, treasures more precious than silver and gold. And then the minstrel's playing ceased, his voice gently was quenched.

The people sat and bathed in the stillness for a moment, and then laughter and speaking murmured across the square. The people began to get up and move away from the square, becoming sparser and sparser. Wendahl stood and watched them, motionless, watching as fewer and fewer people were left.

On nights like this, after the minstrel's playing ceased, when the music finally turned back into silence, he felt a horrible emptiness, a kind of gray nothing that enveloped him and seemed to suffocate all passage of time. He would look up at the stars, but they were like little points of nothing on a thin black lie.

He wondered often if other people ever felt it too, but it seemed as if they never did, and he never asked anyone. After all the people were gone, he sat and watched the embers slowly die out, shivering and watching.

4

The wheat field was full of young stalks that blew slowly in the first breath of summer's wind. The yellow stalks were heavy with the smell of growth and swayed gently in the morning breeze. Old man Cralth stood by Wendahl, his foot standing on a shovel, his hand clasping the handle gently but severely. He spoke roughly and without any sort of kindness.

"Now, I want you to keep this field speck-clear of ravens. The ravens have eaten half my harvest, and if they get a speck more, I'll know who to come for. You can use the stones of the field, I don't care which."

And he was silent and said no more, and jerked his spade from the dirt and trumped away with it.

"Remember - no wheat, no brass!" he yelled behind him.

Wendahl took a stone in his hand and weighed it. The sun was almost born on the far mountains, and brushed the wheat softly with a mellow light. The wheat tossed and turned absentmindedly in a spurious breeze, making a wispy, dreamy sound. A crow alighted on a stalk and pecked, looking at him pointedly from one dark eye. He took the rock and reeled it back, then hurled it mightily. It swished into the wheat. The crow jumped up into the air for a moment, tottering in startled flight, then settled down and pecked again. It stared at him, as if wondering idly what he was doing.

Wendahl looked around quickly and found another rock. He reached down and grabbed it, still cold from the ground. Another bird had come, a raven. He drew his hand back, squinted for a moment, and then chucked it at the far one. It sailed in a perfect arc over both. The birds stared at him in forthright curiousity. He looked around, then scurried and grabbed a few stones, some large and small, and started hurling them at random.

"You stupid birds! Go away!" he yelled insanely.

He ran out into the wheat and charged them, flailing his arms madly. They looked surprised and sailed off, soaring up into the distance. Wendahl bent over, catching his breath and puffing. Slowly he walked back to the edge of the field, stooping to gather a few stones on the way.

By then, a small cluster of birds had come down and began feasting on the tender wheat stalks. Wendahl took a stone and leaned back; he stopped for a long moment, concentrating, then threw it. It sailed awkwardly past a single blackbird and disappeared into the wheat. The birds continued eating. He took another stone and held it a long while, hesitating. He raised it in the air, and held it there tightly.   Then, with a snap, he sent it hurtling in a line. A raven squawked. More birds were coming, and soon the field would be full of them.

Quickly, but surely, he threw some more stones, and a few birds scattered, but not nearly enough. He turned about, this way and that, and grabbed and threw pieces of granite and even dirt clods as fast as he could. It was a losing game, no one could keep up with the bird's hunger, not even with a dozen people. He had one stone left in his hand; he held it for a while, watching the birds feast, his face blank with anxiety. If he was going to win this ridiculous fight, behaving like a ninny wouldn't get anywhere, he could see that by now.

He took the rock and held it up, then waited... Finally, steadily, he threw it. It flew lamely and scared a cluster of birds, sending them haphazardly upward.

The day became like the same dream being repeated over again, but always a bit different. Birds would come, he would scramble desperately to chase them away, and more birds would come.

He found that if he tried to judge the distance too precisely, he would always miss, but if he just threw it suddenly it would hit something some of the time, if he gave himself a moment to aim. By noon the sun was beginning to warm even the hard ground, and his fingers began to ache and spark with distress. The rhythm of the day, of periods of bored, unending dullness when he had chased everything away, punctuated with periods of sudden franticness, lulled him into a kind of half-awake state. He found himself thinking now of many things, remembering, and the day seemed as long as the many years before him, as if he was slowly reliving everything he had ever known over the course of the hours.

But the day had an end, and he was surprised to hear farmer Cralth's voice breaking through to him.

"That's a good job, boy, but I'll expect it to be better tomorrow with practice. I've been watching, don't think I haven't. I suppose it's worth a brassy."

With that, he handed him a dirty brass coin and turned to slowly walk away without looking back. Wendahl watched him shuffle away for a moment, then made his way down the dirt path towards the village.

The sun was smoldering low on the horizon and a bit of wind was coming up. He shivered a bit and hugged himself. The coin was cold and rigid in his fingers, now past pain from numbness, but somehow it felt almost warm.

The wind drove what thoughts he did have now from his mind, and steadily he walked towards the town.

It was dark and smelly in the Black Mongrel as usual, but the darkness outside seemed to make the guttering torch light cheery and homey like a candle in the front window of someone's house. Wendahl took a seat at the front and put the coin down on the counter. The bartender looked down at it without any change of expression.

"What'll it be," he said dully.

"Stew and mead," Wendahl said, his voice tired beyond any emotion, even hunger.

The bartender turned without a word and was gone. Wendahl looked around absentmindedly. The other patrons sat at tables, some grimly enjoying their drink, some talking, huddled in a corner.

The tables were made of old wood and were stained all over with different things. The floors were swept, but still carried pieces of mildewed straw and filth between the cracks. It seemed as if there wasn't a clean spot in the entire place, but it was good to be somewhere warm, away from the wind that waited outside the door. He turned back around and waited mindlessly, staring at the surroundings.

The bartender came back with a bowl of steaming goop in a carved bowl, and a small tankard. Wendahl thanked him rudely and began to shovel the scalding soup into his mouth. It was not the best, with chunks of marsh potatoes and stringy meat, but it might have been Ambrosia for all he knew. After a minute of scarfing like a brute beast, the warmth slowly spread through his limbs, and thought returned.

He finally took a swig of the mead, and its fiery spirits burned through his weariness. The bartender took the brass coin and scattered a few copper mites onto the counter. Wendahl continued eating in silence, and looked around to see if he knew anyone, but no one was there.

5

Farmer Cralth surveyed his fields with a hawk's eye and a cocksure expression, oblivious of the shivering lad beside him. Finally he turned and made an address.

"The same thing today. I'll be back by sundown, and then we'll see whether there will be any brass. Crows are clever. I need a clever boy. I didn't pick that speck-fool friend of yours, he's no good for this work. I know a clever one when I see one. But I don't need a lazy boy. Lazy boys are no good to anyone. I'll be back by sundown."

He turned and walked off, his gait slow but decided. Wendahl took a deep breath and stretched out his aching fingers into the air. They still lingered with soreness, but sleep and yesterday's stew had refreshed him and he felt energized by the crisp air instead of chilled. He walked around a bit, unhurriedly, looking for some good throwing pieces.

Over the course of the days, he slowly gained confidence and soon could keep the intruders away handily, without much thought. He found that he could hit a large crow almost half the time, from anywhere in the field. Soon he walked back and forth by the field like a captain on his ship, now hurtling a stone exactly, now judging the best place for another without even thinking.

Soon the days all melted together, he felt strength coming to him for the first time in his life, and his arms and hands no longer felt the strain of endless use, but felt as if they had an endless well of energy.

He began to recognize the peaks of the mountains and where they lay over the field, and the various dips and features of the horizon, as if he had been there. He found himself recalling the old stories he had heard from the wandering minstrels, just to have something to think about.

The rhythm of the flying stones and the cawing of the frightened birds mixed with the rhythm of the minstrel's song, and with the passage of the sun through the sky, and the deep recesses of the far mountains. When he threw a stone, it was the strike of a sword that killed a goblin, and the protest of a raven became the squealing of an ancient door.

Soon he imagined that he was throwing stones even still, but he was Curdie, leaving them in a dark place, or perhaps hurling them at the head of a bumbling giant, and taunting him as he threw, the giant roaring and floundering. But in the end the squawk of ravens returned, and the stone sank into the wheat field never to return.

6

"I'd wish for some potatoes right now," Colin said simply, his words coming out with a listless sincerity.

"I'd wish for them right now."

He stood by a barrel and looked down at his foot. Wendahl leaned on the side of the building in the dusty alley, chewing on a piece of wheat stalk.

"I've got enough coppers left for at least a moon's tide, maybe," Wendahl said placidly.

The alley was barren, more of a dirt patch than anything else, and a hot, summering wind kicked the dust around into little swirls that chased each other and then went back where they came from.

Colin sort of shuffled along aimlessly, kicking the alley dirt into a puff. Somewhere off in the distance, the shout of someone giving orders to a horse was heard. Wendahl chewed satisfactorily and looked around a bit. Ever since the harvest began, he had been kicked out of Cralth's field, and was looking forward to doing something else, whatever that might possibly be.

He stepped along past the building and stopped, breathing in the lifting warmth of the breezes. There were a few little clouds, but mostly nothing... He continued along, lazily stepping, and by and by Colin followed.

They found themselves outside a dark entranceway, where a gust of heat flowed out sometimes.

"Hey, Derrick," Wendahl called, going in.

It was brutally hot inside the blacksmith's shop, and even the shadows seemed to seethe with a dark heat. The profound clang of weight against weight was heard, and then again, a glancing blow. Slowly, his eyes became aware of a sweating figure, and a bright glow. There was also a furnace that boiled over with rage as the glowing object entered it again.

"I can't talk now, John says so," the figure said, and there was a trace of a wide smile.

It was his good friend, the plain, ordinary boy. Colin came and gaped at the ringing of the iron, and they watched from a distance as he hammered at a small bar. Small pieces came off, little afterthoughts of the heavy blows. "You never thought I'd do an honest job, did you, Wendahl?"

Wendahl shrugged, and spoke up –

"Sometimes everyone must resort to honesty to stay alive."

Colin gave a sad laugh, and they stood watching, the steady working of the boy being the only noise in the room. Soon it was getting unmerciful inside, and after bading a quick goodbye, Colin and Wendahl escaped out through the bright doorway to the coolness of summer.

Everything felt fresh and bright after being inside the smithy. Wordlessly, they continued up the street, letting a wisp of wind dry the new sweat on their foreheads. The sun was tilted a bit in the sky, and a patch of half-shade fell sharply across where they walked. Up ahead, there was a cart in the street, loaded up with some bales of straw. It was lying unhitched in the dirt, and as they passed it, a portly villager came out, busily carrying some mended sacks. He said nothing, and they continued on their way.

They came to a busier part of town, and stood now and then, watching the noise and bustle that went on. There was no hurry, and none was wanted. It was as if the breezy winds of summer blew all time away, so that they need not worry about wasting it. Finally, Colin suggested in a few small words that they visit the Black Mongrel.

It was not as loud as at night in the Black Mongrel, and they went up to the counter after entering. The servingman loomed behind it, a grease smeared apron around him.

"Hey! A potato for my friend here," Wendahl said to the oblivious servingman, putting a few coppers onto the wooden counter.

"Where's your other friend," the servingman asked without interest, staring at Wendahl for a moment.

Then he went to the back of the tavern and returned, carrying a thick hide sack. He set it unceremoniously on the counter and words came out of his mouth.

"The old man with the eye patch says to give this to you. He will be gone for a while."

The large servingman paused, looking somewhat strangely at Wendahl. Then, he shoveled out a grudging phrase from his mouth, "he says use it well", and turned around to work on something.

Wendahl pulled the drawstrings loose on the sack, and reached in carefully. He felt something cold and sharp, and pulled his hand out. Trying again, he felt a leather-wrapped handle and slowly pulled out a long dagger, quite a bit used but freshly sharpened. He held it up a bit, but was unused to holding it and quickly dropped it on the counter with a clatter. Someone in the back of the room laughed hilariously and said something about cutting off a toe, but then all was just noise again. Colin looked over, and smiled wanly.

Quickly he made his way outside, and tried swinging it a little. The blade was heavy, heavier than he imagined, and he quickly realized that perhaps the laughing jokester had actually lost a toe once. The first excitement he had felt was a bit rebuked as he actually held it and saw the keen edge of the blade, so eager to cut anything it touched.

Quickly, he decided to put it away until later. He tried putting it under his belt, and the hilt sat snugly against his waist, if a bit tightly.

Swiftly he came through the streets of the city now, the sword hanging swaggishly on his belt, his feet fit for a king's carpet. It was almost noon, and the air was light with summer warmth and the noise of many people, flocking in different places and making noise, while here and there chickens would come cluttering across the dust of the street and children ducked behind their father's cart.

But no one stopped to look at the dusty boy with an old, gifted dagger at his side, walking along down the middle of the houses.

Now he came up through a wider street into a higher part of town, where the houses were larger and more elegant, and only a few people were out, who turned to look at the boy who came walking past their house, his feet clamping steadily on the harder paving stones here.

He came through a few of these streets and went on, stopping to have a quick wash in a fountain. Now he came to a long avenue, near even larger houses, some with a bit of gardening in front. He walked on as if he knew the way by heart. There was an old friend of his father's who lived here, someone who had been kind to him before. Wendahl smoothed out his chestnut hair in what he thought was a proper manner and stepped politely to the door.

He peered in and could not see anyone. Walking through the entry room, he made his way to the back room where his father's friend sometimes had worked.

The back room was a jumble of empty picture frames and hanging brushes of all sizes and types. The thick odor of paints and wood shavings was everywhere, and seemed to carry a lingering trace of many hours of masterful labor that had gone on there.

Wendahl walked through between everything, careful not to touch anything. His friend sat at a table, working on a length of wood industriously. He didn't look up, and Wendahl continued on.

At the very far end of the room, there was a line of rather large paintings. They were freshly done, and lined up in a row, pictures of various someones sitting at chairs. Each one showed someone as if they were caught in a moment when they were not aware. They were not like the staid portraits he had seen so long ago in his parent's house. Each painting had its own colors that seemed to come out of each of them as they sat there, as if the whole portrait room had been a part of their fleeting thoughts.

The first was extravagant, with many rosy, dainty hues. A young woman sat at a table, her hands folded demurely on her lap, looking at him with a royal bearing, but not haughty or without kindness, wearing a rose pink dress. On the table was a delicate white vase with roses in it. The colors were warm and light, and gently brushed onto the canvas.

The next painting was in varied shades of green, some deep hunting greens and festive ribbon greens, and yellow greens and cool bluish greens that all swirled together in the shadows and outlined a younger woman standing by a table covered with a fern.

She had a bow strung over her lush green dress, and had long black hair that was neatly combed but nonetheless still gave a hint of wildness in its curled ends.

The next two pictures were very much alike, they were done of what seemed to be the same, yellow-haired girl in a room with white furnishings. However, on one of them, there was a sweet, kind expression, and on the other, a silly giggle of mischief. The first wore a beautiful white, lacy gown, and a single lily sat on the table by her. The second wore a pretty yellow and white dress, and had a vase of tulips.

The next painting nearly took Wendahl's breath away. Deep purples and heavenly violets mixed across the canvas, forming a picture of a beautiful girl, her long black hair painted across her shoulders with great detail. She wore a long, violet dress. She had a regal look and held her head up with a bearing that seemed to carry all the breeding of a hundred royal generations. The purple hues blended mysteriously around her, as if she was in a halo of royalty, and a vase of violets sat on the table beside her.

He turned to look for a moment at the last painting, and stopped. Something about it caught his eye after he glanced at it, and he wanted to know why. It showed a slightly younger girl, with pretty red hair, in a nice blue dress. She was sitting by a table with some cheerful red flowers, against some red and blue curtains. She looked rather ordinary, and wasn't very princess-like at all, but had freckles on her cheeks like one of the village girls he had seen around town. Even so, her hair was painted brightly, and it seemed to burn with a fire that came from her very heart and lit up the whole painting with color.

She seemed to be trying to sit still for the portrait, but it looked like she must find it very boring, because she was laughing to herself about something. He found himself smiling about it too, even though he didn't know what it could possibly be.

She didn't seem as calm and demure as her sisters, but she couldn't help it anymore than she could help having such fiery red hair, so she didn't seem very rude either. What a strange girl she was! He wondered why she was looking down. She didn't seem to be very shy, but maybe she thought she was ugly, and didn't want to have a painting done. Really, she's not ugly, he thought, actually, she's actually a little pretty. I wonder if she likes being in such a rich family. It seems like she would find it very boring somehow. If only she would look up, I could tell what she was thinking. But of course she can't look up, it's only a painting. A painting. A sudden thought came to him. Even if this was a painting, somewhere this strange girl was real, living in a large house and with her many sisters. The thought filled him with a strange curiosity.

Wendahl turned around.

"Who is that girl?" he asked.

His friend didn't even look around, but yelled, "Black hair, violet dress, proud expression? Oh, that's Violet. Mm Hm. I knew you would ask! Just forget you ever saw her and you'll be okay."

"No, who is this?" he asked again.

"What? Who?" the friend said, and turned to look. "Oh, that's Karen. She's the youngest. Why do you ask?"

"The youngest what?"

"Of the royal family, of course."

The Royal Family! The knife of curiosity turned in his stomach sevenfold, tightening into frustration. It may as well truly be only a painting. He turned to look at the painting again.

"Well you can't watch those paintings all day, my dear lad, they're due at the castle this evening. In truth, I just sent for some page boys and an escort."

The painting sat there before him, and the girl continued to look down slightly, motionless and still. He stood before the picture dumbly, staring. He wanted to scream, but couldn't, so he just stood there, unsure of what to do or where to go.

Inevitably, time did not stand still. There was a knock at the door, at the front of the house. Perhaps it was a visitor. The old artisan got up slowly and walked out of the room. Wendell heard the opening of a door, and several voices. Then footsteps came closer, and he looked around. Several pages came into the room, dressed in green outfits. Two of them went to the first painting, and very carefully eased it off the floor and started walking towards the doorway. Two others went to the second painting, and lifted it as well.

He began to feel like he should do something, but there was nothing that could be done. Stupidly he watched as the other paintings were carried away, until only the last one was left. He thought of yelling "Wait!" and coming up with some reason that the painting wasn't finished, but it was finished. What a stupid thought. He thought of his new sword, but that was even stupider. Besides, he couldn't even lift it properly, and he would just end up in the dungeon. However, the dungeon was below the castle, and if he could get out, then… what an idiotic thought!! Stupid plans like that could never help anything in a real situation.

It was pointless to even think about it anymore. Perhaps he should just do what his friend had said, and forget about it all. But he couldn't. She was so different from any girl he had ever seen.

The thoughts went through his mind as he watched the painting carried from the room. At last it was empty, and he stood and looked at the wall where they had been just minutes before. His friend, the artist, came up and clapped him on the shoulder.

"Ah yes, Violet does that to everyone. You'll get over her, my son," he said comfortingly.

Wendell thought of saying something back, but any words spoken would be more than useless.

He came back through the streets now, the sword still hanging at his thigh, his steps steady but unhurried.

7

Wendell said nothing of that day to his two friends. He was a great deal quieter, and didn't bother to steal anything. Derrick managed to bring a long piece of iron back from the blacksmith's, and begged Wendell to let him swing the sword, who let him without arguing.

They would take turns with the sword and iron, parrying and fencing a bit, and Wendell always won, although Derrick fought with more furiousness, except for some times when Wendell would get a far-off look in his eyes as if he was thinking of someplace else, and then seemed to be fighting desperately against a hundred men and not just with his good old friend.

They could be heard in the back-alleys of the town, ringing metal on metal, scuffling and advancing, now retreating back through the dust, shouting threats or encouragement to each other.

Some days, Derrick was busy at his work with John the blacksmith. On this day Derrick was free, and the two of them headed up through familiar streets and then to unfamiliar, going by memories Wendell had not thought of since long, long ago, in days that were like the bright pictures of a manuscript, days when his parents still lived.

Eventually the houses began to grow richer and richer, and grew larger to the point where they were more than mere dwellings, but were edifices to the grandeur and splendor of great families. Eventually, he came up a wide, wide street, paved with carefully fitted stones, that he remembered with that euphoric feeling of things long lost.

Turning a bend, it went on straight, towards the castle moat. The castle loomed in the near distance, flying banners that looked like small whiffs against the massive, towered form.

Up ahead, standing in two rows beside the bridge, castle guardsmen stood at attention, their uniforms glistening in the sunlight. He walked up the long street and watched them from a small distance. They paid no attention to him. They had spears topped with a nasty looking point, and looked wearied from their armor.

One of them glanced at him, looking bored. He had a face that looked as if it had seen a few battles, and a proud nose. Wendell loitered about, keeping his distance.

Across the bridge where they stood, there were hedges and a guard's tower, grown over with a bit of ivy. Of course, there was nothing to be done but to sit and stare, so they turned and walked back down the street, and went back to the Black Mongrel.

He looked up now, from the place where he stood beside the Black Mongrel's entranceway. Perhaps she would get bored of staying in the castle and ask to go out and see the city.

She would come and bring her royal servants, and come walking through the street... somehow she would see his dusty clothes and decide to make an example of royal charity, and give him a gold coin. He would bow graciously and thank her so well that she would be astounded, and ask him to come to the castle and meet the king... No. It was an impossible idea.

He looked up. People were milling around, or doing everyday things. There was someone in a brown cloak and hood who walked down the street, someone rather small in stature than everyone else, but who moved with assurance. Now he caught a glimpse of fiery hair beneath the hood, and he walked over quickly to see who it was.

The stranger turned to see who was following, and it was the youngest princess. Quickly he ran over to her, but she looked troubled that she was recognized and started to run away. He started to shout her name, but thought better of it. Then she stopped, and looked around, as if she recognized him, and smiled, just like she had in the painting. Then the dream vanished.

8

Throughout the days ahead, Wendell still wondered about the princess, but had to think about other things. His supply of coppers and brassies was running lower, and the colder months would be coming soon. Sometimes he still imagined how it must be for her, to live in the castle, what she must say to her sisters, but he told himself that it was pointless, and sometimes he could only half remember what she looked like anyways.

He loitered about in the vicinity of the public square, hoping for a likely shop owner to ask him for help, but mostly doing nothing.

This morning, he went there as usual, after waking up from his place under the miller's wagon. It was already a bit late in the morning, and he went along down the dirt path as usual, past the marketplace, and to the square.

There was a crowd of people pressing against each other to look at something, he couldn't tell what it was. He went in among the crowd, and came near the front, where he could see a piece of parchment unrolled and nailed into a post.

"What does it say? I can't read!" someone said, jostling for position.

Wendell maneuvered his way to the front, and one of the townspeople began to read aloud, in a large, husky voice.

"Dear citizens of this our royal city. Greetings, from King Rowan. I regret that I do not have any good news to share with you this day. One of the royal family, my own daughter, has been taken away, while she was in the royal gardens. It is rumored that she was taken to the north, where there is a great labyrinth hidden somewhere among the mountains."

"I have asked my bravest soldiers to go and search out the entrance to this place, but they all refused my command, even on charge of death by beheading."

"It is therefore my plea to you, that if any among you should wish to undertake this task, their reward will be very great, even to as much gold as can be carried away by ten horses, and they shall have their choice of the hand in marriage of any of the royal family."

"I beseech you, that someone among you should carry out their duty towards me and my dear Karen, for I have had no rest and my heart fails me."

"If any among you should not be of a most craven and ungrateful heart, they may approach me at will in the royal throne room, where I sit night and day awaiting your coming. King Rowan."

Wendell stared at the parchment. It must be a dream. Any moment he was going to wake up sweaty and thrashing, and find himself under the miller's wagon as always, with everything like it always was, facing another pointless day loitering in the marketplace, with the princess safely bored in the castle.

He had imagined so many childish, fanciful things about her before, wishing for her to appear in the marketplace. But suddenly those childish things had become soberingly real, and there was no way to make himself pretend she was just a dream now. There was a horrible feeling in his stomach, and he desperately wished he could wake up, but nothing happened.

Slowly, he turned and looked around at the square. He

meandered away from the sign, and watched the people going to and fro, busily going about.

9

Wendell sat on the ground by the miller's wagon in a heap. Terrible things shivered through him. He looked down at his hands, which lay shaking before him. He had never felt so afraid before. If he were standing against some terrible dragon or monster he would simply run away, like in every impossible nightmare.

But there was no nightmare to run away from, nothing but the calm silence of the fields that mocked him. It was a fierce something within that trapped him, which rose up in its hideous strength and hurled him against the fear, even as he howled the nightmare scream of every child before they wake up.

But how could he wake up?? He gasped and pleaded not to face the monster again, the ravenous dragon which twisted inside and told him that his worst fears must come true, have to come true, please don't let her die! But he knew there was no one to turn from, he was pleading with himself, telling himself to forget about it. Let someone else deal with it. Can't you see? I'm only a boy. Please please I can't do it.

We saw those guards. They're dressed in heavy armor. What if they won't let me through? What if they catch me? Don't think of that, please don't think of that, see, we'll just go to the king and he'll say no and then there's nothing else we can do, yes do think of it!! See, it's impossible. Let's just go back to the Black Mongrel. What am I saying?! She can't die!! I still remember... don't think of it... no I have to!! Who cares about the guards?? I'll cut them to pieces! I'll beat them into dust!

No, their spears are so sharp. What if they caught me sneaking past?! I'd have to fight them, or get thrown in the dungeon!! I went there with Derrick, and I saw them. If we ran up to them then, they wouldn't even be afraid of us!! No no I remember her face so well, she was laughing about something, it made her so happy, even though she was so bored from sitting still, what could it be?... why did this happen, I don't want this to happen... I'll just forget about it all... there's nothing I can do... how can I say that?!

No, we're going to go. We're going to go up to those guards and go to the king, one way or another. I'm so afraid. I'm so afraid. I can't do this. This isn't real. This all can't be happening. Why did this have to happen? I can't believe I'm going to do this.

10

"You're crazy, Wen."

Derrick shook his head in agitation. He chewed on a piece of wheat feverishly and spat in the dust.

"You're absolutely crazy. I've known you since... I've known you a long time, 'nd you're the slyest one I ever met. But you're not all great, you know. Not that great!"

Wendell stared at Derrick's head as it looked down at the dirt in the deserted alleyway.

"You don't care, do you? It doesn't mean anything to you!!" he spouted irately.

"I don't know what you're talking about, Wen!! We're a couple of street rats!! What do you want me to do, go march off into the forest at random, probably get eaten by wolves on the first night? What do you want me to say??"

Wendell's chest burned, and he braced against the shame. He had decided to tell the plan to his best friend, and now that the secret, precious thoughts were laid bare, he felt stupid and useless.

"If you only... if you had..." he stammered.

"Forget 'bout it. I don't want to lose you, Wendell, you're a good friend!! Can't you see that? Why are you doing this?? John even asked about you. You could be an apprentice too!! You could have a real job for once!"

Wendell looked at his friend's turned away face, his own face twisted with frustration. Without a word, he turned and walked out of the alley, never looking back.

"You're crazy! You hear me? You stupid bastard! *That's what you are!!*"

The voice faded away and then finally stopped.

The dagger was where he had left it, wrapped in a torn piece of sackcloth. It was heavy as ever, but somehow now all the weight was like a dull itch that he didn't bother to notice. The streets were the same as always, and he went through them quickly.

Now he came to the wider, more prosperous streets, where the houses rose higher and more elaborate, and the streets were clean and paved with perfectly fitted stones.

He turned a bend, and at the end far ahead the castle sat, huge and looking down indifferently on all the houses, the great royal banners flying like handkerchiefs from the parapets. He made his way up the middle, step by step, along the wide road that stretched out long into the distance.

Finally, the dark specks of castle guards became larger, and every now and then he could see them say something to each other or fidget in the hot sun. They stood in two rows, one on either side of the bridge. Now the plumes on the top of their spears and helmets became clear, the bright red sometimes flashing bright in the sun, flapping listlessly in the breeze.

Inevitably he reached them. The main guard put his spear out sideways to signal for him to stop.

"What is your business, lad?"

"I've come to see King Rowan," Wendell said lamely.

The guard looked at him with a bored, irritated expression.

"About what?"

Wendell's mind squirmed with indecision. He felt like a chicken asking a wolf to eat her. But he stood up tall and tried to sound grave.

"The proclamation says that anyone can come see the king."

The guard gave a spiteful sort of snorting laugh.

"You're just here to see what you can steal, aren't you?? Get out of here, you little runt."

Wendell's face burned with rage. He went right up to the spear, and stuck his finger at the guard.

"It said anyone could come!! You have to let me pass!!"

"I said get out of here!"

"You can't just... ! You can send a soldier to make sure I don't steal!! I'll leave my sword behind!!"

"Is that what you call it?? Go or I'll throw you in the dungeon so long you won't even remember your own name!!"

Wendell's eyes stung with acid. He formed mouthless, irate words at the guard's stony face, and clenched his hands until they were sore. He backed up a few steps, never turning around. Finally he turned and looked back down the road. He was about to take a step and walk away, but somehow it was the end of everything. He would be walking into that thin black lie which had smothered the sky every night after the minstrels sang.

He knew it was utterly pointless to try to pass the guards, but every time he tried to think of leaving, disgust and horror raged through him until he forced it away, as if he was crushing something innocent beneath his foot with each step. He spun around and shouted at the guards.

"I don't care if you throw me in the dungeon!! I'm staying right here!! I'm not going until you let me pass!!"

Wendell waited for the inevitable. He was suddenly aware of how stupid he sounded, and that he wasn't wearing anything but a ragged tunic and leggings. But he didn't budge.

The guard looked somewhat amused beneath his distemper. He had had a boring week, evidently.

"Very well. We'll see how well you do without food. Or water. If you're still here at the end of two days, I'll let you pass. But you can't leave, even for a moment."

Wendell looked at the head guard and nodded grimly, his face smiling an awful, joyful smile.

The hot sun bore down mercilessly throughout the rest of the day. But Wendell had stood outside all day before, and he didn't even have to chase away any ravens.

He wiped away the sweat that trickled down from his hair. He walked back and forth before the guards, just like he had always done, and sang the minstrel's songs. He sang about

David, who sat by the sheep killing bears, and wasn't afraid even of a giant. He sang about the great warrior Ren Zael, who fought death itself and stole the keys of the underworld from the great dragon!

He sang until he was too dry to make a noise, and then his chapped lips formed the words. Finally, mercifully, the sun went down, and the guards changed, clinking away wearily in their armor. The head guard talked to the new leader, who nodded gleefully and looked at Wendell.

By now Wendell's head ached, and his whole being trembled for the coolness of water, drowning out any semblance even of hunger or tiredness. At last, he lay down on the hard stones and curled his arms over his head, and passed fitfully into a horrible half-sleep.

The sun beat down warmly and gently, casting a red glow through his half-closed eyes. Wendell slowly eased himself up to a leaning position, and looked around puzzledly. He saw the guards, and he realized what was going on again. Determination twisted in his stomach, overpowering the deplorable thirst that throbbed in him. He stared blankly at the guards, his mouth working uselessly.

He sat and waited on the ground. All he had to do was wait for one more day. One more day, and he could go see the king.

The guards passed around a skin of water, gulping down chugs of it manfully. One of them looked at Wendell pitifully, but Wendell just shook his head weakly. All he had to do was just sit and wait and wait. Just sit here and watch the guards, don't move, and you can see the king. The king! The most powerful one in the land. Surely he could help. The king could help him.

He remembered a song he had heard, something about "I'm going to see the king". He mouthed the words listlessly. Somehow it helped to sing. It made the fitfulness of hope grow stronger, as if the ones of old who wrote it had been here in their own days, sitting and waiting. He felt somehow that he was singing the very secrets of how they all succeeded, that he was singing them all now, even though he didn't hardly understand what those secrets were.

But saying the words and notes made him feel that he did know the secrets after all, and for a moment he forgot to worry and knew only of their terrible strength and hope, as the notes rose so pure and full of hidden glories. But then he would think that it was just a feeling, and so hope withered back to a dying stump.

The sun came down in an unrelenting torrent that threatened to scour away all thoughts and consciousness. Wendell was lying away from it on the ground. Feebly, thoughts and feelings still trembled through him, and a vision of the well and bucket came unremittingly to him. But all he had to do was wait!! Just lie here and wait…

Wendell woke up the next morning, not remembering the previous evening or night having passed. Something cold hit him, and he started up, only to flop down again. It was water.

"Have a drink."

The voice was almost familiar. He looked up, and the face of the head guard looked down at him, somber and disgruntled.

"It's the third day. Have a drink."

Wendell reached up, his head swimming. The water skin flopped on the ground, and he grabbed it and poured water all over his mouth and his face, wincing violently as the water touched the dangerously chapped skin. After a minute, the water soaked in, and he began to feel almost alive again. The guard looked down at him, then began laughing. He laughed on and on, more uproariously now, and Wendell wondered if something was wrong.

"It was all a joke!!" the head guard said hilariously.

"The king can't be bothered with silly young knaves. He's too busy. You can go home now."

It took a moment for his mind to piece together the words. Then he staggered to his feet, and dizziness took over. He had only a few moments to think of something, anything. He looked over, and saw a group of trees beyond the last great house before the castle.

He wandered over to them, and took refuge in the shade, the guard laughing behind him. He sat at the back of a tree, his back to the bridge, and took stock of nothing, because there was nothing to take stock of. He was so tired. So tired. There was no way he could even swim across now, even if he found a way. There was no way he could fight them off, even if he could fight. There was no way he could do anything.

11

It was wonderfully cool and dark. Darkness was in shapes, and there was a bright glob of light, so bright and wonderful, never moving, between the dark shapes. Cool soft things that brushed you with friendly fingers, nice happy sounds that didn't want anything but to be dark and happy.

Wendell slowly became aware of what he was seeing. The moon was peeking through the trees, and he was lying on the grass, listening to an owl somewhere above. Then he remembered. The bridge.

He was much refreshed now, but that just made him aware that he couldn't do anything. He thought about getting up, but there was nowhere to go. He sat up out of habit, and looked at the moon unseeingly.

The slow dawning of truth was like the tying of a horrible knot he had seen in a picture once. It was the only thing that mattered, and the only thing he could do nothing about.

But the moon didn't move, and the trees stayed where they were. He was free. He could go anywhere, do anything he wanted. The thirst had not killed him, and he could wander down the streets and find a life anywhere, anywhere in the whole world. But the taste of freedom was a glob of staleness, and he didn't bother to think about what he should do.

Wendell got up and walked to another tree, then turned and looked back. He walked back to the other tree. A cool breeze came up. A faint whiff of happiness went through him, but it stung like a whip. A few weeks ago he had been happy, happier than he had ever been, in his life.

Why couldn't it be that way again? But he didn't want it to, it would be an even worse nightmare than the miserable knowledge he clung to. It would be a nightmare of happiness, where the terrified cries of a lost girl would be lost forever, never even reaching the ears on his silly, grinning face. He shook his head, and looked up blankly at the sky.

A bank of clouds inched across the moon, leaving behind a speckled patch of black. The stars were still beautiful tonight, even if nothing else was, so very far away that their endless light was pressed and lost in the darkness until only the purest diamonds of brightness came twinkling through.

Everything in the world was ugly and empty. But the stars were his own sorrow, beyond all reach but still right there, and even though they were so endlessly far away, still they wept with him and knew what he felt.

He didn't know quite how it had happened. He began to speak - not singing the songs, but reciting them, rambling on, as one recites a poem, until he was almost shouting, finally giving vent to all the rotting hope inside, with the words giving meanings to his own thoughts that he didn't even understand.

And now his voice was David's voice, was Curdie's voice, it was Ren Zael's voice, and he forgot for a moment that he was just Wendell the street urchin sitting in a clump of trees looking at nothing.

But the words ran out. He stumbled over them, desperately pressing against the fear that would come, trying to think of something, anything.

He couldn't stand to be idle any longer, just standing to stare at the motionless trees that didn't care about anything and didn't move. With a horrible cry he threw himself down on the ground in a heap, weeping and clutching at the dirt. He wasn't even sure that he even believed in the gods. But he believed now, not because he believed it, but because he had to believe it.

He remembered he had heard once that Ren Zael was the son of a god, so he decided haphazardly that he would be the best one to believe in. It was a stupid decision, but nothing made sense any more and he really didn't care.

"Ancient Father of Ren Zael, you must help me... I will always serve you always, if you will help me!! I don't know even how to serve a god, but someday I will learn. I will give up stealing, if you will help me now!!"

He didn't feel anything, no reply. Not even a breeze. But the words of the songs still burned on his lips, and so he kept on.

"Yes, thank you for helping me! You must be truly great indeed, to have helped Ren Zael and Curdie!"

And he laughed, the tears running down his face, spilling into his idiotically laughing mouth.

A terrible thought came to him. Did he trust this god at all? Did he believe that they would help, or was he just messing around, because nothing was left to do?? He brushed off the thought, and was silent, looking for more words. But he could remember no more. He went to the edge of the trees, and looked at the guards standing in the moonlight, not noticing him.

He thought again, "Do I trust them?" Finally he stopped and thought about it. There was no way for him to know if they existed, or if they even could hear him. Was everything just a lie then, was his life just a stupid story that was over while he was still alive? If there was no god that could help him, then it was just all a lie. Nothing he did or said anymore mattered. The whole world may as well not even exist.

He tried forcing himself to understand things, to believe that the stories of Ren Zael were true, but it didn't work.

Everything around him was the same as it always was, there were no magic creatures to ride here, no secret powers to find in a hollow tree stump. Just him, sitting in a clump of trees, waiting for nothing.

But then, he thought, if it was all just a lie, then why did it all exist at all? But it did exist!! Why did the princess live, if she was just going to die?? Why did he live to see her, and to love her so much, if he couldn't do anything about it?? He found himself looking at the stars again, because they at least understood him. Their light was just a little song, tiny and beautiful even though they were just a mistake.

He didn't know what they were singing about, but he understood it more than anything he had ever heard or seen before. They were singing a song of love, a love pure enough that it kept on loving even after it didn't even matter anymore.

They were singing a song of hope, a hope so strong that it kept on hoping even after hope itself was already gone. They were singing a song of faith, a faith so trusting that it let itself be beaten to death before it would say that the killer was unkind.

He remembered at once an old man's voice, speaking words – "Heroes of long ago… who by some hidden way, discovered their destinies and made us remember the way things were made to be… Life can sometimes seem like a broken story, wandering, pointless, and without end. So much so that we can almost forget that it ever was a real story to begin with, and that there ever was anything good and true in it…"

Things were meant to be like the songs, he understood now, to have something good and true in it. But could they be? Or was all the hope inside him just like the singing stars, swallowed up in an endless sea of darkness? "By some hidden way…" What was that hidden way? If he could only know the hidden way that they did those things, he could do it too. But he didn't know. Not even a clue. But he had to!

He got up from the ground, and paced between two of the trees. He laughed and clapped his hands together, defiantly against the sorrow and fear that still churned horribly within. Now he crossed his arms. He felt his hopes harden into iron within him.

Now he walked out from among the trees, and made his way near the bridge. The main guardsman came out to meet him.

"I told you to go away..." he said, his voice dangerous.

Another soldier came walking up towards them. Wendell felt the urge to get away as fast as possible, but he just stood there. He was about to speak, when the other soldier raised his spear. Wendell closed his eyes and winced.

"Let him pass, Altross. You gave him your word."

The other soldier's words were deadly serious, with no sign of wavering. The head soldier turned and drew his spear, facing the other. Wendell sensed a hesitation, and ran straight ahead for the bridge. The soldiers parted for him, some giving a grim smile as he passed. He didn't look back.

There was a row of hedges on either side leading up to the castle gate. The portcullis was down, and there was a single guard standing in front.

"I've come to see the king!!"

His words seemed to jolt the soldier out of his stupor, who shouted up words to someone. The portcullis slowly ground open, and Wendell stepped inside hurriedly as the wide gates swung open. There was a long hallway ahead, with other hallways branching off on either side, made of massive stones covered by rich red tapestries. The floor was spread with massive red rugs. Moonlight shone through a high opening, lighting the way.

A voice called out behind him, "Intruder! Don't let him in, you hear me? *Don't let him in!*"

He never looked back, but went down the hallway to the large doors, bursting them open with two hands. There was more hallway ahead. He was already weak but he ran on, the muscles in his legs dying.

He slammed open another pair of doors, and ran onward towards a great portal, with two very officious looking soldiers in front, their spears held in an X across the door, which was emblazoned with a huge, royal emblem in the shape of a tree.

"I've come to see the king! You must let me in!!" he panted hoarsely. The guards looked hesitant, but stepped aside. Before they could even open the portal, Wendell had already run his shoulder into it with a horrible thud, pushing it open an inch. It finally swung inwards, and Wendell came tripping into the room. His sword clattered onto the floor before him, and he fell headlong in a heap.

He was up in a moment, and saw the king sitting ahead of him, and two guards, elaborately dressed, moving towards him, their huge spears lowered and ready. Wendell grabbed the sword and held it out before him.

"*Stop!!*"

The king's voice echoed throughout the whole chamber. It was a very large chamber, with enormous tapestries hanging everywhere, all with the same red symbol on them. There were columns in two rows leading up to the throne, which sat at the top of many steps.

The soldiers looked at each other, and went back to their positions. Then Wendell looked at the king.

The king had dark, horrible circles under his eyes. He was sitting up now, his hands gripping the sides of the great throne. All his skin was pasty white, and an untamed beard sprouted from the deathly paleness. His expression was made of acid.

"What do you want?" the king spat out, his mouth chewing the words.

"I've come about the proclamation."

The king burst into a fit of agonized laughter, looking around at the guards, who kept their spears pointed at Wendell.

"The procla... *the proclamation!!*" he squealed, and laughed some more.

Wendell didn't know quite what to do.

"A thousand brave men in the kingdom, and this is the only one who shows up. What are you, about fifteen years of age?"

"Yes."

"So tell me, boy, what is your plan? Do you know, you are the very first person to even enter this throne room since the proclamation went out?"

"I am not afraid anymore, your majesty."

The king put his head in one hand, and leaned, his dark eyes fixed on Wendell, his expression terrifying.

"I suppose if I did send you out, it would be murdering a child. But you're the only one who showed up so I don't have much of a choice."

"I can tell by your entry that you must be very brave. And that you snuck past the guards. I'll speak to them, most likely from the other side of a guillotine.

"But," he chuckled ruefully, "if there's any chance, even a slight chance that you might succeed, then, well, I suppose I don't care if you die."

"I understand that, your majesty."

The king looked a little ruffled.

"But what about your own life? Surely your life is not without any meaning?"

"I do not understand my life, majesty. I never have, and certainly not now. I do not know whether I have found a meaning or a purpose for life. I only know that a purpose has found me, and I must follow it, or else nothing."

The king looked at him, a bit of the dark humor gone out of his face. He spoke more soberly.

"Those are very large words for one so small. Do not mock the things of eternity, for they rule us all, whether we know it or not."

"The question of whether life has meaning is for those who are not faced with despair and death," Wendell said darkly. "I only know that I must go. There is something terrible inside me, and if I do not follow it, it will never end."

The king stared at him, his mouth flat.

"Very well. I will let you go, boy. I will send my very best men to help you search the entrance to this maze. From then you must go on alone.

"That is, unless you can persuade them to go with you!" he laughed joylessly.

"If you are to succeed, then you will become blessed above all your wildest dreams."

The king bit off the last words like a curse. He motioned flippantly with one hand, still leaning on the other.

"Provide suitable quarters for him. Bring me the Generals."

One of the guards came down from the steps and took Wendell's arm in his large hand. He led him out of the throne room. After a few turns, he opened a strong wooden door with a key on his belt, and gestured for him to enter.

It was the grandest, most extravagant bedroom he had ever seen, done in reds and blues, with a great goose stuffed bed and a large window with real glass, and large bear skins covering the floor.

"Someone will bring your dinner shortly."

With that the guard was gone. Wendell looked around. Ordinarily, he would have been delighted just to be in the castle as a guest, and to stay in such a room, but now he hardly even noticed. A great and terrible hopefulness was rising up that he hardly dared to touch.

He still hadn't really done anything yet, but he knew now that he wasn't completely helpless. He wasn't as stupid as the bridge soldier had thought, after all. He paced the floor and looked out the window again and again, completely unsure of what would happen tomorrow.

12

A great light appeared. Voices singing. Something thrilling and delicious filled the air. He became aware of a kind, wise face. A beautiful face. Then a pair of wings, and hands. She spoke gently to him. She knew him. She knew what he was doing.

"I am Danala, the great queen. You don't know who you really are, do you?" she said, smiling wisely.

Wendell shook his head confusedly, still in awe of all the light around him.

"Oh, my child. The stars sang on the day you were born. You are the perfect one. The brave and true. I will go with you on your journey, and give you success."

The words were so simple, yet they seemed immensely profound as she said them, as if each word were a deep jewel of eternal meaning.

"Be strong, my child, and remember what I have said!!"

"But... how can I be perfect? I know I've made mistakes. I... stole things. I lied to people. I hurt my friends."

He found himself speaking in the plain, simple manner of the fairy.

She laughed, a high, soaring laugh.

"The perfection is within you, my child. It will come out someday."

Wendell nodded and smiled.

Then she rose up into the air, and her laughter faded away into the morning light.

13

Wendell blinked and smiled. What a wonderful dream. The light of the sun came into the room, lively and steady. He slowly got up, and looked around at the room. All the horror of the past days seemed to be gone, and he felt almost cheerful now.

There was a knock on the door. He slipped out onto the floor, and padded over to the door, and opened it. A page boy came in, bearing an immense tray of all kinds of food, muffins and apples and hot waffle cakes and steaming drinks.

He remembered that he must be hungry, and that he should probably eat something, which he did, thanking the boy before he left. The food was very good, much better than anything he had ever had before. The steaming drinks were filled with all kinds of spices and flavors that he didn't know the names of, and the muffins were soft and delightfully chewy. His stomach was glad to have food, even if the rest of him didn't much care.

He stuffed the food down, and before he knew, it was almost gone and he felt somewhat stuffed. A delightful thought came to him, which quickly turned sour. The painting! The painting was here!! He wanted desperately to see it, but the mere thought of standing and seeing her with his own eyes again was too much to even think about. He looked at the last bit of food, but he felt too jittery to finish it now.

Another servant came to the room, with a message.

"You are to go to the royal gardens, where the general will instruct you."

When pressed for more details, the servant shook his head dumbly. Wendell followed him down the corridor, and through several more, remembering to take his sword with him, which had been lying on the bed with him. Finally they came to a nicely wrought gate, which opened easily. Through it, the beginning of the gardens was there. There was a clearing of grass, with some small trees at the edges.

Beyond, he could see some hedges and rose bushes laid out in a neat pattern, and beyond that, walls and arches. There was no one there at present, so he sat down in the shade of a nice apple tree and waited. The garden was pleasant, and there was nothing to do, so he found himself thinking about the dream.

It was true!! He would find Karen after all. He smiled and closed his eyes. The stars all sang when he was born, and he could not fail. He was the perfect one.

"You're not perfect."

He looked around, startled. It was a man's voice. It sounded ordinary, and was matter of fact, without malice. At first he thought it was a gardener or something, but how would a gardener know what he was thinking?

He looked around everywhere, but there was no one. Now his good mood was completely disheveled. He put his head down and tried to think about something else.

The general came out from the gardens, striding with a military assurance that had long ago graduated to swagger. He had an eye patch over one eye, and was chewing on something. Wendell stood up, and started to wave, but the general saw him already, and met him in the center of the grass, which grew wild here and was still covered with dew. He smiled swaggishly, and

Wendell got the impression that he was in a sort of good mood, but he was not one to be trifled with. It was still early in the morning, and the air was still fresh and bright with new sunshine.

"Well you certainly don't look like much. I heard about how you slipped up my guards. That must have been a nice piece of work. I should punish them for letting you get past, but I'm already punishing them for not letting you get past. Maybe I'll punish them for both."

He gave a laugh, with a thin layer of friendliness in it.

"I had to do it. I'm sorry, sir."

"Just call me Hangs." he said, clapping Wendell on the back. "I wish I had more soldiers like you, brave as a marsh pig and just as stupid. So you had to do it. Well let's see how you handle a sword. If you get caught next time, you'd better know how to swing that potato peeler of yours, or you'll end up in the dungeon for longer than I can remember. I suppose you should get a better sword, but you're already used to that one and I can't teach you all over again in a day."

Now the general drew his own dagger, which was about the same size as Wendell's. He had another sword on the other side, a real sword. The general spat out whatever he was chewing, and took up a position, holding the dagger in a way that made Wendell's blood run cold at the sight. He slipped his own dagger out of the belt and held it out in what he hoped was a menacing way.

The general dropped his pose and walked over to him.

"No, no, no!! You'll get clobbered at the first strike holding it like that. That's not a real sword, it's made for parrying, so it should be used defensively."

Hangs took hold of his hand and arm, moving it into a different position. It felt strange and he wasn't used to it, but he tried to memorize every angle. Now the general moved Wendell's arm slowly through a sweeping arc.

"That is the first defensive position."

Now Hangs took his position up, and held up his dagger.

"Now do what I showed you."

Hangs gave a sort of half-hearted jab at Wendell, who clanged his own dagger down on it furiously in the way he had been taught. With lightning quickness, Hangs made a step forward and stopped his dagger on Wendell's throat.

"Control is more important than power for defense. You must divert the attacker's force, not overpower it. Try it again."

Wendell tried the move again and again, each time receiving comments, some appreciative and some very disparaging. It was hard work, and he was surprised at how difficult it was to do this simple block. In the back alleys, fighting against Derrick, his own determination and improvising was all he needed to win.

It was good to do something, anything, and he welcomed this task. It brought a numb quietness to his raw nerves, and the garden's stillness was a gentle balm, broken only by the ringing of steel that faded suddenly into the trees.

The most frustrating part was having to painstakingly think through every single muscle bend. He always imagined himself pushing back impending armies with great, cutting swings. The general seemed to be able to fight without even thinking, always coming out with a new, more deadly attack just when he thought he was safe.

Now the general stood back a bit.

"I suppose we're done for now. Good job, kid. If it were up to me, and it isn't up to me, I'd train you for a lieutenant and forget about the king's brat."

The general's words shook Wendell for a moment, but they only reminded him of who he was dealing with here, and that the world he had entered now was not a kind place.

The general turned and started to walk away. Now he turned suddenly and leaped at Wendell, who brought his dagger up stoutly, and the general's weapon was glanced aside. Hangs grinned a wide, dangerous grin for a moment.

"There's hope for you yet, boy. If you make it back in one piece, I'll make you a lieutenant if you're not too busy. Violet is quite a handful, even if she is beautiful."

"I don't care about Violet, okay!! Just… Karen."

The general glanced around at him, amused, and he laughed a chuckling laugh to himself, as if he knew something. Wendell wondered what he was laughing about. But soon enough, the general was gone.

Now that the lesson was over, he felt quite tired and sore. He was alone in the garden again, but somehow he didn't feel like just sitting and resting right then. He went back through the decorative gate, and through an entrance to the castle. He realized, after a while, that he was wandering through the castle grounds, lost in a sort of half-thought.

Now he came to something like an informal gathering room. There were some elegant white curtains hanging for decoration, and some chairs, as well as a white couch. He wandered into the room, when he realized who was there. It was Violet, in a luxurious violet dress, lounging over the couch. She didn't see him.

For a moment he was startled, because he only knew Karen and her sisters as motionless faces in a painting. She was humming a listless, lazy, bored, wandering tune, and snacking on a plate of some kind of cakes.

Now she looked up, and looked as if she had seen him every day of her life. Now Violet was very pretty. But she just smiled a cool, amused smile.

"You must be the boy they're talking about. It's very brave of you to go fetch my sister. You'll choose me, of course. They always do. My father tries to bring princes to meet my sister, but once they see me, they never look at her again. She cries about it later. She denies it of course, but I hear her, in her room. But I'm not worried, a little boy like you will never make it back from the labyrinth."

Wendell spoke up indignantly.

"I'd choose Karen instead of you every time!! She's the most wonderful, beautiful girl that ever lived!! And she has a beautiful heart too, which is more than I can say for you, you stuck up witch!!"

Violet sat up now, in a fit of regal, girlish rage.

"So that's what you think? Well, she's crazy anyways!! She's always going out into the garden to talk to her imaginary friend. It was cute when she was little, but now it's getting kind of old."

"She's not crazy!! You're just telling me lies!!"

Violet seemed pleased by his outburst. Now she leaned back, as if purring.

"You'll find out soon enough. That is, if you make it back."

Wendell clenched his teeth against the fury. He started to speak, but turned and saw two other girls standing at a doorway. He recognized them as the yellow-haired twins from the paintings. One of them looked at him with a concerned, sad expression, and the other giggled and covered her mouth when he saw her. The kind one spoke first.

"It is very good of you to go and find our sister," she said sincerely.

Then the other one piped up.

"Yes. Don't mind Violet, okay you nice boy?" And then she giggled again and ran off.

He decided there was nothing else to be done, so he turned and left.

Now he went through the hallways again, but this time he had no idea where he was. Eventually he found a servant, and snapped a question about where his room was.

The servant looked startled, and quickly led him along. He finally made it to his room, and the servant opened the door for him. He threw himself onto the bed and sunk into a deep, restless sleep, filled with hallways that never went anywhere.

14

The next day there was another lesson with Hangs, as well as the beginnings of horse riding. Fortunately, Wendell was not heavy and the grass was soft. By the time they were finished, dusk was falling.

The banquet hall was large and noisy and well-lit, much more than the Black Mongrel ever was.

A monstrous dining table somehow carved from the heart of an enormous tree went down the center of the long room, and was decked with shining silver goblets and gold plates, steel knives, candles, and ivory cups.

At one part of the table to Wendell's left, Hangs sat with his best generals, laughing bawdily. At another part, dignitaries and high officials sat and conferred politely. Wendell himself sat at the very end of the table, next to the king's own plate. Across from him was an empty chair.

King Rowan bashed his fist on the table and talking ceased. It was very quiet. The king stood up, and everyone hurriedly rose also. Wendell rose awkwardly from his chair last of all. The king surveyed the men at his table with a look that was terrifying.

"I would like to propose a toast..." he snarled humorously, "to the bravest, most able-blooded man in the kingdom."

Everyone uncertainly raised goblets, and then lowered them awkwardly.

"I have made it a point," he went on jovially, "to surround myself with the fiercest of men, of unswerving loyalty, who would surely strike *fear* into a traitor's heart."

He went on as if drunk, but with an icy edge under his voice.

"But this toast, is not for them. Not even for Hangs, my cold-blooded general, who fears not death. Not for my cunning chancellor, who fears no poison blade. No, no! Although they fear nothing, they also have no fear of their ruler."

"So it is, that I propose this toast to a mere youth."

He raised his goblet, and all the others followed.

"And so toast him this day, all of you - he that risks his life while you stay safe in the castle like silly sheep, toast this lad who keeps you drinking rum - while he goes on to certain doom."

He ended with a giddy stagger, raised his goblet and took a great swig.

"*Drink!!*" he roared.

Rowan sat down, and everyone followed hastily. He looked at Wendell with a kind of courteous face.

"So my dear boy, whatever caused you to do all this?"

Wendell did not feel much like talking about the painter's house, but he thought it wise to humor the king, who was busy dismembering a large chicken.

"You see, your majesty, I know the royal painter."

The king gave a painful snort of laughter, his mouth still chewing meat. He turned to Wendell like an old chum.

"I see. I see. That explains it. You know, we still have the paintings here. You may see them any time you wish."

"I... I don't want to."

"*Why not?!*" the king snapped.

Wendell didn't know what to say. The king went on eating furiously. Finally Wendell said something to keep him happy.

"It would... remind me."

The king mulled it over. He fixed Wendell with a steely, scheming look.

"You will see the painting. That you will."

Wendell felt his stomach rise with a deplorable happiness. The king went on.

"Young blood won't boil forever! If it helps you fight better, I'll lock you in there with those paintings until you go mad! Don't think I want to see that painting any more than you. I know! I know."

King Rowan rose from his great chair and gave an address to one of Hangs' friends. They escorted Wendell out of his chair and to a door. The last thing he heard as the door slammed was the king's mad laughter as it echoed throughout the giant chamber.

15

The portrait wing of the castle was silent. It had a long, long hallways, with wallpapers of light red, well-lit now with torches on the walls opposite the paintings. Wendell was led to a door, and inside, there was the beginning of another hall, shorter this time, and painted with fine whitewash, and hung with other paintings.

He looked at the first one, and recognized it as the first one he had seen before. A flood of old memories poured in, and for a moment he felt just like he did on that day, the carefree lad who had just gotten his first dagger for his birthday and walked proudly down the street to his friend's house.

But then the memory faded, although it still hung around him like a sickly sweet scent, a smell of innocence and forgetfulness. Against his will, he looked slowly from one painting to another. Some paintings were a bit different than he remembered; others were the same, but his eyes saw them differently now. At last he could no longer avoid the last one.

He only saw it out of the corner of his eyes, burning with red, as he looked unseeingly at Violet's pose, but he still recognized it. Without thinking, he looked over.

For a small moment he forgot that anything was wrong. She was still sitting in the chair, with the cheerful red flowers on the table, looking down a bit, and laughing to herself, just like before. Her hair burned with a fierce, dreadful red, and flowed down her nice blue dress.

Her hands were folded in a pose of awkward demureness on her lap that seemed a poorly done imitation of her elder sisters, and it made Wendell want to laugh. She looked down a bit, and her eyes carried the sweet scent of something, lost in the shadows of her glance. She giggled to herself, and Wendell wished to know what could possibly make someone so happy? It was a riddle of joy, as if she was a sad girl who had a single happy thought, just as the painter looked up.

Then he remembered, and his happiness became stone. He wearily turned away from the painting and tried to think, but all his thoughts were like sad feelings and his feelings were like bitter thoughts. He hugged himself and forced something through his mind. He was hardly even fifteen. What was he doing here, in this castle, going out to do what? He wasn't going to find her. All the soldiers in the kingdom couldn't find her. Maybe she was dead already.

He looked up, and saw her hands, trying so hard to look gentle and peaceful. She should never have been born into such great royalty!! She should have been born to some farmer. He chortled a little, and a few miserly tears found their way to his mouth. It was ridiculous. Why was he so happy when he saw the painting? It only made him remember these horrible things.

He had tried to think so soberly, to realize the gravity of the situation. He needed so much to turn away from the painting, to be reasonable, force himself to prepare for reality.

Tomorrow he would leave the castle, and go out towards the north, but from there he didn't really know what he was supposed to do. He knew his way around the common areas of the woods, of course, but not anything further... what is she laughing about so much? It can't be something stupid, like her favorite pet or a joke. It seems like the most wonderful thing in the world, something that you could whisper to anyone sad, and they would cheer up.

16

Wendell sat and stared at his plate. The king looked over.

"No appetite, eh? Good, good..."

He didn't feel like answering. At last, the king stood and clapped mightily.

"I would like to welcome a guest tonight. The master storyteller *Garim!*"

A hooded figure at the far end of the table got up slowly and put back his hood. He made his way to a chair beside the massive fireplace. Now he threw his arms out and spoke commandingly.

"I am the simplest of all things, and so even a child can find me. Many know my name but never find me. Others, find me without knowing what they found!"

"I can be found anywhere by anyone! No one can see me, no matter where they look."

"I always succeed in what I do."

"I am not fire, but no flood ever puts me out. I am not water, but no wall stands against me."

Wendell did not know the answer. But as the storyteller spoke he felt his heart burning at the sound of the words, as if he had known the answer all his life and just remembered it. But the riddlesome words were cold and unyielding in his mind. Like an old padlock that refused to budge, no matter how he fiddled with it.

"Whoever can solve this riddle can know much! And whoever cannot solve it knows *nothing whatsoever.*"

"No one can solve this riddle unless they need to with all of their heart. For those who are simple, I am clear, but for those who are clever - *I am cleverer still!* To those who are listening, I listen, and those who laugh at me, I laugh at! *Ha!*"

With that, his cloak fell back around him, and he collapsed into the chair, saying nothing. The king's face was lost in wandering thought.

The words of the riddle were marching grimly in Wendell's mind, never letting down their masks of meaning, and for some reason he wanted to know the answer more than anything, it seemed so obvious for some reason, even though it was so absurd!

But he couldn't figure it out. It was a distraction from other things, but not a comforting distraction because the more he thought about it the more impossible it was to have an answer.

His thoughts were frustrating.

"Air is everywhere, but it was not clever or... how did it go?"

Back in his room as he tossed to sleep, Wendell's mind was full of floods and fires and invisible nothings that had no name, that swirled and roared about a red-haired girl wandering through a maze.

17

The next morning there was a rap on the door. After a moment he remembered where he was, and everything that was going on. He was going to go searching for the labyrinth! Wendell sat up and looked all around the room. Everything still looked exactly the same as the day before, as if nothing important was about to happen.

There was a servant at the door with some clothes. Wendell took them and went back into the room, and laid them on the bed. There were expensive riding boots, and a fine cloak and a skillfully woven shirt and lots of other useful things.

It would be time to leave very soon.

After getting into the new traveling clothes, he was led quickly from the room. It was so early in the morning.

Several tired soldiers came out and mounted up onto the horses, as well as Hangs, who looked around fiercely now, with no laughing humor left. Lastly, the storyteller came out as well and got on a plain brown horse.

Wendell shook the sleep from his head, and awkwardly got onto his own horse the way Hangs had taught him, after a few tries. His horse didn't seem to care about anything and put up with his efforts.

Without a word Hangs pulled on the reins, and his warhorse stepped into a ponderous walk. The other soldiers and Garim followed, and Wendell last of all.

Hangs spoke roughly, his face serious.

"Well, this is all your plan, so tell us which way to go."

Wendell didn't really have much of a plan before. Before he had dreamed so much of going before the king and finding help. But now he looked into the endless trees and felt a bit of sad anger that he still seemed as lost as when he was all alone.

"We'll go to the north, through the woods that way," he said, pointing with one hand and holding onto the reins tightly. He remembered that there was a woods path there, and would lead them a long ways into the forest before it ended.

The long line of horses went South across the castle moat. They kept walking at a steady pace, while the misty edge of the forest grew closer and closer.

Wendell looked closely at Garim for the first time. The face was older but he still recognized it.

"You remember me, don't you?"

The storyteller looked over quickly and a wry smile went up on his face. Then he spoke, as if he had known Wendell all his life.

"Somehow I knew it was you as soon as they told me about you. Yes, of course I remember you."

Then he looked a bit puzzled for a moment.

"What is your name again, lad? I never bothered to ask."

"Wendell, sir."

The storyteller nodded.

"Wendell... wanderer... searcher... seeker... a fitting name."

"So what's the answer to the riddle?" Wendell asked eagerly.

"The answer? What are you wanting me to tell you, a word? A name?"

"I don't know." Wendell hadn't really thought about it.

"I don't know completely what the answer is," the storyteller confided.

Wendell looked at him uncertainly. The storyteller continued.

"Knowing who someone is, is more important sometimes than knowing a name for them. Just like I forgot your name, but still knew who you are. The riddle is its own answer. It's what you do with the answer that matters."

Even though he still felt cheated, the storyteller's commonsense answer put Wendell's mind at rest somewhat. It made some sense, he did know all about whatever it was, just from hearing the riddle. He tried and tried to picture something... adding one part of the riddle after another. But the picture always fell apart long before the end. "To those who listen, I listen." Listen to what?? The riddle?

No, everyone could listen to the riddle, but not everyone would believe that such a strange, fantastic thing could exist! What you do with the answer... what are you supposed to do with it?! It didn't make any sense, but the more he thought, the more familiar it all was somehow like hints of a forgotten dream.

"Are there any more riddles about the... answer?" Wendell ventured.

Garim smiled.

"Your question shows that you know more already than you think you do. Yes, I believe all good riddles and stories are about it."

His answer made no sense, but Wendell realized that he expected such an answer, and he knew it was the right answer. All stories! He had heard many stories, but they were all about different people, different things. But they were all good, faithful stories, and it brought him much comfort to think about them now.

Soon the woods lay directly ahead. They made their way among the shadows of the trees. Soon they reached the forest path and were going much faster than before.

"Which way should we go now?" Wendell whispered hopefully to Garim.

"You don't know??" he whispered back, amazed.

"The Labyrinth is in the North, of course! It is said - the entrance is along the Aelahna pass, although that is purely a *rumor*. Of course the labyrinth itself is purely a *rumor*," he said matter-of-factly.

"Of course, the only thing we're sure is not just a rumor is Karen herself, and most girls don't just disappear into thin air."

"How can I even find the entrance? What does it look like?" Wendell whispered too sharply, feeling worse.

"How did you do anything so far?" Garim said straightforwardly.

"I don't know! It doesn't make any sense."

"Well if you don't know how you did it, at least you know *why*. That's a lot more than many people figure out."

"That's not very helpful!!" Wendell snapped. "I'm being serious here!"

Garim let out a long breath and looked up ahead.

"So am I," he said grimly.

Wendell looked over at him with confusion, and Garim continued looking up ahead. Now he was left with his own thoughts, which were not much better than talking with the crazy old coot.

The riddle, the stories, the songs, the old man's answers, they taunted him, burning in his heart without letting go of their secrets. For a moment sometimes he would listen to them, to wish that they were all sensible, and they raised his hopes in a terrible way, and made him feel that anything could be possible.

But he still didn't know what he was supposed to do at the end of it all, and he wished for once that someone would say something practical and just plain to understand.

It was as if all reasonableness had vanished from the world. But this was no joking story, it was a deadly game, a tricksome nightmare that he couldn't ignore or escape from. How could all these things help him, he thought? Maybe he should just let go of that nonsense. He let out a deep breath. The storyteller continued watching the forest.

Yes, he needed to craft a reasonable plan. Such as, well... first of all... there was no reasonable plan!! No one had the slightest idea where Karen was, and the possibilities were endless.

He ground his teeth together and wanted to howl with frustration, but he just hunched in his saddle. What kind of monster would create a situation like this?! But he had no one to blame!

So the road continued steadily onward, and Wendell was left with his own thoughts, that marched around like a nonsensical parade of deadly grimness.

Eventually, they came to a break in the woods. They continued along, coming now to a pass going up a long slope. Then the steep pass split in two.

One part was going upwards, and another sloped down gently to a quiet woodsy place. Looking up at the other branch, he could see a dark ugly sky in the distance, with large black things flying in circles beneath the clouds.

"No, we won't be going there. The lonely wilds is not a place for young lads, even if they are brave as a marsh pig," Hangs said in an almost fatherly sort of way. He pointed at the lower path and smiled smugly.

"That's the Aelahna pass, down there."

They went down the slope carefully. It was a very beautiful path somehow, even though if Wendell looked at any one rock or tree or patch of dirt, they all looked the same as any other he had ever seen, but there was something beautiful about the place anyhow.

Soon the pass flattened out, and went among the trees, curving this way and that way, sometimes going past patches of grass or flowers. One little patch he saw through the trees was a vibrant shade of red, and it reminded him suddenly of something. The flowers seemed to burn inside with a deep redness, and it made him catch his breath at the sight.

He never knew there were flowers like that anywhere! But soon they were gone, and there must be more further along the path, probably closer. Perhaps he could pick some to give to her, when they finally...

But as they went along, all the other flowers were rather ordinary, and he wanted to go back and find the others. But he gritted himself up against the thought. There was no time to pick flowers now, we need to... the thought ached in his heart, panging against his will, and now he wished to go back, just to see the flowers once more and be reminded of her in some way. But they had to find the entrance! It could take all day to find, or many days...

"Okay. Where do we go now, boy?" Hangs asked with no politeness.

"Back that way."

Hangs looked surprised at his quick answer.

"Why?" he asked sharply.

"Because of the... I saw something." Wendell felt extremely stupid, and wasn't sure if he could dodge much longer.

"What?" Hangs stared at him with honest puzzlement.

"Never mind," he said reluctantly. Garim glanced over at him, but continued looking on ahead as they plodded forward.

18

The caravan continued its journey through the woods. Wendell tried to think clearly, but the farther they went along, he felt more and more miserable until he couldn't stand it.

"I don't understand," Wendell blurted out. He looked over at the storyteller.

"What don't you understand?"

"All of it. Anything. Everything you've said. Everything that's going on. The stories, the riddle, the songs... what is it all talking about?"

Garim looked at him soberly. "What? You seemed to understand everything well, but now you don't understand."

"You know what I mean," Wendell said wearily.

The storyteller looked down a bit, sadly.

"Oh."

"I mean, I wish someone would just tell me what I'm supposed to do. I wish someone would just be straightforward, be clear and simple."

"Maybe we are being clear and simple..." Garim said sardonically.

This answer was even less satisfying than any of the others. Thoughts went through his mind, heedless of his attempts to ignore them. "I am the simplest of all things, so that even a child can find me." What a useless riddle!! "I always succeed in whatever I do. I am not fire, but no flood can put me out..." Wendell stopped in his thoughts. It always succeeds. That would be a useful thing to have!! Perhaps it was a magic dust that was invisible. But any child could find it anywhere... how?? There was nothing clear and simple about any of it!!

All he knew was that he must find the answer. That's all. But the answer was in the riddle, and the riddle was the answer, and... oh, who cares?

But he couldn't not care! There must be something he could do... unless he could find it, and then he could do anything!!

He laughed sadly at the ridiculousness of the thought. He slumped wearily in the saddle. He would do anything to know. Anything. Okay. Maybe the riddle actually is clear and simple. Yeah!! What am I saying?? But I have to try!!

He licked his lips and shivered. "Maybe we are being clear and simple..." the storyteller's words rang in his head. Now what? There was no way for him to understand.

"I am not fire, but no flood can put me out." He imagined it, a fire that no flood could put out. He imagined a fire burning, and then a bucket of water falling on it. The fire went out. Another fire, this time hotter... it ate the water mercilessly. Now he sent a huge storm wave against it. The fire in his mind blazed hotter and brighter, until it became his own heart's hopeful despair.

"I understand!!" He blurted out loudly. Hangs looked at him strangely, then turned back around. Garim looked over at him suddenly, surprised. Then he smiled and went back to looking at the road.

Wendell remembered... the flowers!! A burst of hopefulness went through him, at the memory of their lively red color.

"We have to go back!! Stop!!"

He pulled up on his reins, and his horse whinnied in protest. All the horses stopped.

"Back that way!!"

"What? What is it?" Hangs asked, reeling his horse around. The other soldiers gathered their horses near.

"Just follow me, okay..." Wendell said hesitantly.

"Wait, what is it?" Hangs spouted.

"I... there were some flowers. Red flowers. I wanted to pick some."

Hangs gave him an impossible look.

"Well, you're the leader here," he said, shrugging carelessly.

Quickly Hangs turned his horse about and Wendell's horse followed. They retraced their journey quickly, and Wendell looked nervously to see if he could find them again. The other soldiers looked too, looking a bit sheepish. But the patch had been rather far away, and obscured by trees. There was so much forest to see, and little bits that came and went from view. But at least now he had something to look for, to find, anything!!

"There!!" he yelled, pointing. Hangs turned in his saddle and leaned to look, then grimly led the soldiers onward, handling the reins expertly. They came to the patch, which was rather small, and Wendell dismounted quickly, almost falling backwards into the grass. Fortunately, he knew more about falling than riding.

"I thought those only grew in the royal gardens. You've got some eyes. Now, go pick your... flowers... and let's get back to the path before evening. The wolves will be out."

Wendell got down and picked one. They looked so alive, he was afraid to even step on them, but he wanted to keep at least one. He looked around. There was a small clearing farther into the woods, with yellow sunlight brightening it, and more trees on every side. It looked so cheerful, it made him want to smile, even though he was so sad inside.

Without thinking, he got up and walked towards the clearing, and heard the others following behind. He stepped out into the open from the shade, and the sun felt so bright after being in the woods all day, and for a moment his dark mood began to melt.

But he couldn't help it, even though nothing could make him happy before, but the sunlight's warmth seemed to seep even into his bones. What a strange thing, he thought. I bet this place could make anyone happy, no matter how sad!! Just like... Karen's smile!! She was thinking of someplace like this, I suppose. He just stood in the sunlight and didn't know what to do next. One of the soldiers was talking, but it was far away...

No, it wasn't a soldier. He listened more carefully, and it was the sound of running water, a babbling brook. Where was it coming from? He headed off through the wild forest plants towards the noise, stopping to listen often. The soldiers and Hangs and the storyteller came behind him, watching him silently. As he came closer, it grew louder and clearer, but never turned into a roar.

There was a clump of bushes ahead... he shoved the branches aside, holding them back with each hand and slowly stepping through. He came through and there was a bustling brook running down a jumbled streambed right on the other side. It sounded like brooks always do, as if they were trying to say something but couldn't make up their mind what to say first, so it came out as nonsense.

But he liked to hear it anyways. Now what, he thought. Is this another... something like the flowers and the sunshine?

The brook continued babbling, but he didn't know whether to go back and look for something else. Maybe the babbling would make sense. He listened, but it just sounded like water. He stood there and watched, and heard the soldiers getting restless on the bank. Oh, I have an idea!

He looked for Hangs.

"How does... how did Karen's voice sound?" Wendell asked, trying to smile a little, as if it was a casual question.

Hangs hid his distaste for the question beneath a dutiful expression. One of the soldiers spoke up, though, looking off into the forest.

"I never heard her talk very much, to be truthful. Except of course when she was out in the gardens, and then I could hear her sometimes, far away, talking to the trees or something. Her voice was a lot like the gardens, I guess, kind of wild and quiet at the same time, meandering a bit, but sometimes it was like... she wasn't really talking, she was just being silent out loud. I don't know. Mostly she could be pretty quiet. Then again if she got angry you could hear her across half the castle."

Wendell felt a bit of a tear coming to his eye at the man's simple, elegant words. He listened to the brook intently now, which was noisy, but still didn't disturb the quietness of the forest.

19

Wendell walked quickly up the slope by the stream, stepping carefully over the stones on the bank. The soldiers clinked wearily after him, as did Garim and Hangs. Eventually he reached a small embankment of rock, which had a cave-like opening where water poured out. He could hear the water burbling far into the blackness.

"We must go in there," Wendell said assuredly.

Hangs looked into the darkness, his face emotionless.

"We should probably set up camp for the night for now, the wolves won't wait for us when it gets dark first," he said, a bit of his old humor creeping into his voice.

The task of "setting up camp" was something Wendell had never had to do before, certainly not with a group of soldiers. He always simply went to sleep under the miller's wagon, where there was old straw to lie on, and somehow it was strange to be in the forest at dusk, so far away from there.

When he started gathering branches, Hangs stopped him and said he had orders that Wendell should "save his strength for the journey".

So he was left to listen to the soldiers foraging, and the distant cry of a wolf or two, and to stare into the mouth of the opening, trying to see if there was any hint of another side, or mostly just trying not to be impatient and bored while staring aimlessly at a black void. At last the soldiers had made a decent camping fire and some piles of leaves and brush on the ground.

The sky soon darkened tremendously, and they were lying around the fire, the soldiers wrapped in their cloaks and sleeping. Wendell was vastly sore and tired from riding, but he found it difficult to sleep. Garim lay on his side, asleep in his traveling mantle, and one weary soldier held watch, looking patiently into the forest.

Wendell faintly heard voices. He must have fallen asleep. The voices were serious and busy discussing something. Slowly he opened his eyes to the frozen forest air and saw Hangs and some other soldiers standing in a cluster, in the firelight. One of them saw Wendell awakening, glancing at him with a wary look. He sat up now, and blinked, trying to wake up and figure out what was going on.

"... came all by itself, without any pack members, and didn't make a single noise. It wasn't the least bit wary, and never even whimpered when I stabbed it."

Now he recognized Hangs' voice, low and deadly.

"... care what it was. From now on, two soldiers will stand watch. I can't go back to the king and tell him that his pet was eaten by rabid wolves."

He looked around for the first time now. The mouth of the cave was still there, with the stream gurgling out of it, just like before. Hangs walked over to him, as did Garim and the soldiers.

"You were almost wolf chow last night, boy," Hangs said with a sardonic somberness.

He had no reply, but was thankful now to have Hangs and his best men around, even if they were so coldblooded and harsh. In all his meager plans he hadn't thought about defending himself while sleeping, and he tried to push away endless images of a wolf sneaking through the darkness after him, that seemed more real in the freshness of morning twilight than they would as a fireside story.

At dawn they cleaned up the campsite, after a breakfast of dried meats and cheeses, as well as strips of an unknown meat that were roasted over the embers with a few sticks, giving off a potent smell. One of the soldiers handed him a piece, and as he chewed warily, he was informed that "wolf isn't all that bad, eh?" He decided not to eat the rest.

"Which way now?" Hangs asked plainly, looking about.

"We should go in there," Wendell said assuredly, pointing into the black mouth of the cave, which poured water down into the stream.

Hangs seemed to be thinking it over.

"An opening like that no doubt leads to an underground spring," one of the men said. "There is no point in exploring.

Before we reach much further, the cave will be neck-deep in water."

"He's right. Let's move on."

Wendell stood, and stared at the blank opening. It wasn't large or small, but rather round. Water poured in a discordant rush from it to the streambed a few feet below.

"I... I think we should go in there," he asserted.

Hangs gestured towards the cave.

"Very well, you first."

Wendell walked into the streambed, being very careful on all the slippery stones. Eventually, he reached a hidden dip forming a small pool under the opening, and waist-deep iciness rushed steadily around, dragging him backwards. He felt with one hand in the waterfall and reached a protruding rock, but the unceasing torrent pushed on his hand and made it difficult to get a steady grip.

Painstakingly, he felt a ledge with his other hand, and dug his fingers into it tightly. Now he pulled himself up, and put one foot tentatively on something, perhaps a twisting root... his handholds were squeamish and slipping, but gently, gently, he climbed...

He fell backwards with a wail and splashed into the shallow water.

Soon he was trembling with chill and fatigue, as he carefully chose each stone to climb on, his fingers numb and shaking as they grasped the quivery stones. It was maddening! The opening was right there, just a few feet in front of him, and all he had to do was climb a few silly rocks.

He always imagined that perhaps he would have to fight some horrible creatures, and he bristled with eager fury at the thought, but he never expected such an inane, senseless chore... what was the point of it?

As he climbed, thoughts went randomly through his mind... "why am I so sure the entrance is here? Because of some flowers? A stream? Why would that be a clue? But if it is a clue, who left it there? Maybe Karen dropped some seeds!! But how would they sprout so quickly? And what about the sunshine? It doesn't make any sense!! Oh, watch that left hand... easy... easy..." Splash!! He got up and tried again.

He had made it almost to the top again... he reached up and clung desperately to the watery surface of the opening, his fingers wavering violently, but he concentrated on tightly, gently holding on... he closed his eyes, and took a deep, shuddery breathe. If someone, something had left clues for him, then he must be able to make it up. A tremor went through his soaked frame. Who could be able to leave such clues? He had no way to know if he could even trust them, whoever they were.

Horribly, slowly, he pulled himself up, his teeth clamped painfully, and reached inside... he felt a sharp rock jutting up, and eagerly grasped its raspy surface. He clambered in, and deep breaths of exhaustion came out, and he rested there for a while. But he couldn't stop for long, he needed to reach the other side and dry off quickly...

Wendell crawled ahead, stopping every few seconds to reach ahead into the shapeless void and watch out for pieces of rock hanging from the ceiling. Soon the tunnel turned a corner, and he saw bright sunshine at the other end, which sloped upwards a bit. But he was too cold to yell anything back to anyone.

Crawling out now, he was too tired to even look around, and lay on the ground facedown, feeling the warm sunshine on all his soaked clothes. The grass was very soft, and smelled of rich, warm earth.

Finally, he got up and looked around. There was a clearing, and the stream continued to the right, onwards into some more trees, which were taller and different than the ones he had left behind.

He stooped and yelled into the tunnel.

"I've found the other side!! There's some more trees here!! Hey!!"

He waited a little. There wasn't a reply. He tried shouting a few more times, but soon ran out of voice and had to stop. Wendell sat down on the grass and looked around, more closely... the woods were rather peaceful here, and there was nothing unusual about them that he could see. The trees had leaves that were a slight bluish-green color, and spread their branches majestically into each other.

At another time, it would have been quite a comforting place, if someone else was with him and he wasn't trying to find anything. But all the peacefulness made him want to do something, and he got up and walked around, trying to form a kind of plan. But the plans didn't seem to get that far.

Something else was crawling out of the opening... it was Garim! He wheezed and threw himself down on the ground by the stream, his hair dripping softly into the dirt.

"Are you alright??" he asked concernedly. Garim gave a grunt of agreement, and then clutched at the grass wearily.

Someone else began coming through as well, a soldier, who also flopped down onto the ground. Wendell waited, but no one else appeared.

20

"I don't think I've ever seen this part of the woods before," said the last remaining soldier. It was the one who had spoken of Karen's voice by the stream, and Wendell felt very glad to have his company. The three of them continued by foot, walking steadily between the trees that grew mutely in the green of forest twilight.

"It would be best to stop here for the night," Garim said now, looking around. "I don't think there are any clearings to be found."

There was no fire this night, and they huddled miserably against trees, trying to find comfort in a piece of moss or some trampled foliage. The soldier took the first watch as the other two struggled to fall asleep.

Something was shaking. It was his shoulder.

"It's your turn to stand watch," said a tired voice. Wendell sat up dismally and tried to be alert, watching the nothingness all around him. It was beyond all darkness now, and Wendell felt his ears pricking up at the faintest traces of noises in the woods, many which he could not recognize. Things rustling about far off, and small breezes, little snaps and ghostly whirls of noise... how far away, he could not tell. Something crinkled, then stopped. Two intelligent, wolfish eyes looked at him, unblinking. He sat up and tried not to breathe. The eyes looked back at his, calm and inquisitive. Then they turned away and moved noiselessly into the depths beyond sight.

21

Eventually it was Garim's turn to stand watch, at the beginnings of dusk, and Wendell gratefully went back to his miserable spot on a mossy tree root. It was barely morning when he was awakened again, and soggily got up and began walking around to loosen up his stiff legs and arms. His empty stomach gnashed itself horribly, but a dull excitement still lingered, drowning out thoughts of food.

After a meager breakfast of soggy cheese and some rather sour berries, they began foraging ahead through the trees, no one saying anything. Wendell slashed at branches idly with the dagger to pass the time, but despite the endless urgency inside he felt a sickly boredom creeping in.

He found himself seeing how far he could look off into the distance between the trees, and every now and then he saw a distant object move, perhaps a deer or large rabbit.

The woods seemed so plain and quiet in the day, not at all as he had pictured them when he went before the king and demanded to go on the search, full of horrendous, grasping monsters and certain death, or huge packs of snarling beasts. It was more like a long picnic walk.

Once or twice he thought he saw a large, husky wolf somewhere between the shifting trees, standing alertly, its ears pricked up, looking towards them, but when he looked again he couldn't find it in the endless maze of branches and trunks. It sent a brief chill through him, and for a moment he wondered if he hadn't been silly to wish things weren't so quiet. But inevitably he began to think of it as a friend almost, and when it was gone he wished it would appear again so that he could have some company besides everyone's endless footsteps and the other's silence.

That night they settled down to another dismal sleep, taking turns at watches.

22

Wendell sat watching the endless night, that lingered on into the distance. It was so lonely, alone with his thoughts, that churned horribly like his hunger. If only there was someone to talk to, but even if Garim was awake he didn't even know what he would say to him.

But he must stay awake... he had almost been eaten before... it had come, silently, stealthily, before opening its mouth...

Eyes appeared again, from behind a tree, and moved noiselessly towards him, lucid and rakish looking. Wendell held up his breath and made sure his dagger was still in his hand where he had left it, trying not to move even a hair. But of course he had to breathe, and heard the tumultuous rush of his own breath.

The eyes seemed to be looking directly at him, and he didn't know how long he stared into them, wondering when the thunderous rush of fur and teeth and blood would come, and whether the others could wake up in time to save him before he was torn apart. He thought of calling them to wake up, but he couldn't budge himself while the eyes still stared at him, so wild and intelligent. Finally, calmly, they moved away and disappeared.

In the morning, Wendell said nothing to anyone, but hunger was beginning to make him light-headed and dizzy, and only a throbbing nervousness kept him on his feet, pushing him to walk onward. Garim even rambled a bit, some old stories about foxes and wells and candlemakers and such, but they didn't seem interesting at all. Those stories were always so tidy and complete somehow. He looked out for the wolf almost eagerly, even though when he saw it it still scared him. But even that was nowhere to be seen.

Finally, Garim suggested they rest for "lunch". They stumbled ahead a few more steps, and then stopped. A huge, gray shape moved out directly in front of them and sat, holding a very fat rabbit in its teeth, snuffing its breath in and out. It was as tall as Wendell even as it sat, and the soldier hurriedly drew out his sword ahead, but it didn't seem to care. It padded up to Wendell and dropped the ball of fur at his feet, then trotted away. No one said anything. Wendell poked at the dead rabbit with his foot, and finally the soldier spoke up.

"Well... who's hungry?" he said in a kind of encouraging way, giving a sort of smile.

After scrounging for a long time, they managed to scrape together some decent brush, and a while later than that the rabbit was roasting and crackling juicily on a spit. Everyone took turns taking pieces off, each with their own dagger, but no one said anything. Wendell thought of making some sort of comment, something like, "rather nice of the wolf, wasn't it?" but it always felt stupid if he opened his mouth to say it out loud.

That night Wendell watched anxiously for eyes to appear again, during his stand at watch. It gave him something to look for. Inevitably, they did appear, and looked into his eyes for a long, long while, so fierce and solemn. He stared back, trying to understand what the wolf was thinking.

They seemed to be such noble eyes somehow, and sometimes he almost thought they might be faithful and trustworthy, but then he always remembered the rabid wolf that had come for him before, and so the eyes became merely wolfish and wild again. When they finally left, he was left to endlessly argue with himself, whether the eyes had indeed understood what he was thinking the whole time.

23

In the morning, Wendell sat up, again, as he had so many mornings before. It was becoming something of a daily ritual, the waking up and walking about, and then setting off into the woods again. Garim and the soldier got up too, breathing fog into the air.

Today, no one said anything as they walked. Wendell looked about through the woods, and often saw the familiar gray shape of his "friend", sitting alert and watchful.

Trees made way to more trees. An awful queasiness was forming inside, and hunger and tiredness gnawed through him always. Finally they stopped for the midday rest. The soldier and Garim hung their heads wearily and leaned against some trees, still never speaking. Wendell paced about haphazardly rather than sit down.

They had been walking for four days, or was it five? He had heard once that a strong man could make it for thirty five days without food... they had dew for water, and an occasional stream. But I'm just a boy, he thought. Surely the labyrinth can't be more than another week away... they could all make it that far.

He looked off into the trees, and tried to make out anything in the distance, some sort of marker to judge against, but all was just more and more forest.

Finally he stopped walking. He glanced back at the way they came, then quickly looked away. If only there was some way to tell how far I've come... maybe I could climb a tree. But I don't need to know how far to go back yet, of course, only how far until I reach it... even if I have to walk here, for the rest of my life...

Wendell sat down and hunched against a tree. The gentle sounds of the forest came and went around him. He looked up... the wolf was there again, sitting a dozen paces away, calm but very alive. The wolf stared into his eyes, looking so grand and inquisitive, but Wendell hunched up against the tree even more and put his head down on his knees. The wolf's panting breath continued, never wavering.

A horrible feeling spread through him, and he tried to drown it out, rocking a little. He looked up again at last, and his gray friend tilted its head to one side, in a doggish way, pricking up one ear. Wendell wished the wolf would just go away, but now he couldn't tear his eyes away from the dumb animal's fierce gaze. It was just a wolf. It couldn't tell what he was thinking, the eyes just looked that way because wolves are naturally clever or something.

The wolf looked back at him, never moving, never angry or proud. Wendell felt himself speaking to the wolf without words, softly struggling against the brutish beauty of a face that couldn't hear or understand him. He gave a sort of withered sigh. The wolf padded towards him, and began licking his face in a playful way with its hot tongue. Wendell tried to gently push it away, but not too much, or it might get angry and bite him... he heard himself laugh as it licked him. The wolf stopped licking and stared at him uncomprehendingly, panting happily.

The wolf licked at his tears now, and Wendell always remembered that for some reason the wolf's rancid breath smelled sweeter than anything he had ever known.

24

    That day Wendell convinced them to follow the wolf down a pass to a lower place, where they found a huge river swarming past. There was a very small, leaky boat lashed to a tree stump, and when Wendell got in, the wolf suddenly stepped in behind him and sat patiently. Wendell looked back at the others, but Garim merely said, "The time for the help of men has come to an end for you, it seems." Then there was nothing left to say.

Wendell strained all his meager strength against the unfeeling torrent, using a flat, pudgy oar that was left in the mucky bottom of the tiny boat. Every now and then some bitterly cold water splashed his face and hands, and was left there until some breeze would come up and dry it off.

Soon the desperate chore settled into a numbing rhythm of weariness against power, and if he stopped for a moment the current would suddenly send the little boat spinning downstream, almost out of control. The wolf sat behind him noiseless and out of sight, but he still felt its presence, and he was dearly glad to have something with him right now, even if it was only a wild beast.

He often expected to hear Garim's voice suddenly making a pithy comment as he rowed, something profound about perseverance and the candlemaker who never gave up.

But then the wind suddenly hushed over the sharp splashes of his oars and he couldn't find anything else to hear, to listen to, not even the rustling cloak of the soldier turning to look at something. He looked up ahead, and the sky was tormented with a blackening inferno that wailed in silence. He wondered how many days the silence would be there to counsel him and help him, but there was no one left to ask.

Finally, he dragged the boat up onto a pebbly shore. Up ahead there were more trees and woods, looking rather nasty and vicious in the dusk, but Wendell was sure that they would look fine again in the morning. After searching for a while through the pitch-dark forest for some firewood, he finally curled up against a tree and shivered into sleep.

25

In the morning there was nothing to do but get up and search about. Half the time he was about to turn to Garim and make some sort of suggestion, and then he realized he was alone, of course. The wolf returned, and Wendell paced into the forest again to find some berries.

Soon he could no longer tell which way he had come. Eventually, Wendell was surprised to find himself walking through the dried husks of a once mighty forest.

Through the trees in the far distance, he thought he saw strange-looking rocks now and then, but it was hard to tell whether he was imagining them from so far away.

As the strange rocks grew closer they grew weirder looking, but they were still were somehow familiar! There were shapes almost like creatures, but it was impossible to tell where the head or body was.

There were many large, tilting lumps that looked almost smooth. And there were square, rigid stones, tall and severe. Even though he didn't know what they were, they seemed to have a horrible meaning to their forms, as if someone put them there to keep people away. Or even anything that was alive.

As he stepped out among the rocks at last, he realized that he was walking through the deserted remains of a graveyard, probably abandoned for hundreds of years. Up ahead the land sloped sharply upwards, and a ledge of crumbled stone blocked his way. At the very top, was a little wooden door.

Wendell stepped cautiously through the stones, and the wolf didn't notice anything, but kept following him. He reached the base of the ledge, and found that rocks had been weathered into a path, twisting back and forth up the slope. Eagerly Wendell and the wolf meandered up, listening intently to the silence, but there was nothing. Finally, doubled over with tiredness, he limped up the last few steps, and hugged himself against the freezing wind that poured down from above the rocky ledge.

The door was made of a sturdy-looking, hearty wood. It was larger than it had looked, and perfectly round, set into the stone exactly like some kind of jewel. There were weathered decorations on it, patterns of gilded gold that might have been letters or pictures once. They almost swirled around the door, chasing each other in eternal dances of yearning and impossible perfection. For some reason Wendell knew what they meant, although he couldn't even begin to tell himself what, and they terrified him with delight and sadness to see them, as if they were about to crumble and fly away into the air, gone forever.

It was here! The labyrinth, after all! But of course it is, he told himself, or why would I not have gone on for so long? But he could give no answer to himself. He reached now for the latch, but it wouldn't open, even as he tried rattling it in different ways, forcefully and then gently. Then he noticed a tiny keyhole under it, and slumped down against the door...

"There must be a key of course," Wendell thought. "Whoever made this door wanted people to get through it, of course... or they wouldn't have made a door... that would be pointless!"

There was nothing left but to wearily make his way back down the slope, step after step, and look through the whole graveyard one stone at a time. The wolf followed Wendell around while he looked. It sniffed the ground sometimes but never seemed interested in anything.

He stopped to rest a bit, leaning against the icy surface of the wall, and tried to think of who made the door, and where they might have put the key, and why they would leave it locked it for so many years. It was probably in a safe, safe place, clutched by the bony hands of some long-dead monarch, far beneath the ground. Probably one of the larger monuments would be the first place to look.

There were so many graves, and he didn't even have a spade to dig with. Any other time it would have been creepy just to be among so many tombs, but now he didn't really care.

Wendell shut his eyes and tried to block out the fears that were coming. If only there was someone to help me, he thought. The wolf could dig, but he didn't know how to ask it to, of course. If only there was someone who knew... please please...

He started to get up now and smacked his head on a twiggy branch. He reached up now, and felt something cold brush his hand, and pulled it back sharply. Then he reached up again, and felt it again, hanging from the branch, a thin object with bumps and...

He laughed nervously and started up, hitting his head on the branch again. Now he reached up and felt the key again. It was hanging there all the time, ready to be found by anyone who needed it. But why would it be in such an obvious place? There must be a way to keep any random person from finding it. But who really cared! He had found it!

Wendell's feet felt cold and unsteady, but he eagerly stepped through the graves again, ignoring how exhausted he already felt. The door was getting closer, and it would soon be wide open, and he would see the labyrinth at last! It was true!

The wolf pricked up its head now, looking off into the distance, but there was no time left to stop. He heard a strange noise.

At first he thought it was the wind. But it was different. It wasn't grinding, or slithering, or the sound of distant thunder... in all directions, like the wind, but slow, and horrible, and growing louder.

There were some sort of grotesque leaves trembling on the ground before him now. Or were they a stick? Then the sticks wriggled in the dirt, and some more white things pushed up through the crumbling earth. Was this a horrible weed?

The weeds were growing up quickly all around, one before of every stone, everywhere. Wendell tried to quicken his steps, stumbling along hurriedly, but almost tripped himself.

Now the wolf stopped and growled brutishly, pulling its ears back, ready to throw its immense weight into a pounce. Wendell stepped into a dazed half run, keeping his eyes on the path ahead. He heard the rattling of something metal now, and as he looked back there were swords emerging from the dead soil, pieces of armor and helms.

Behind him he heard the wolf snapping and growling. It was the dead, clawing themselves out of the ground, with nothing left but their bones and battle armor. Wendell tried to hurry as much as he could.

The long, turning slope that had been so gentle before was impossibly steep now, and Wendell needed to rest, had to rest after reaching the first corner. He collapsed into a heap, panting furiously.

There was a muffled sound rising, of feet marching in unison, and ancient armor jostling in a tinny, hollow echo of military unity. There was nothing left to hide behind, nothing but hundreds and hundreds of little pebbles on the ground.

The footsteps were marching up the slope, steadily, feet that would never grow tired. Wendell stared into empty eye sockets and the bottomless grins and slowly pulled himself to a standing position.

The dagger that once seemed so heavy and dangerous now felt like a child's plaything in his hand, laughably weak.

He had felt such fury and despair once, when he first heard the king's proclamation, and Wendell remembered how he imagined again and again and again that he would cut down everything in his way, while fighting with Derrick in the back alleys, and standing before the king, or practicing with Hangs, like he would do if he ever needed to!

Now it was time. He was going to find himself smashing through all their brittle bones any moment now, just like he always had! His hand clenched weakly on the dagger's hilt at the thought, and a boiling tear of outrage and frustration stung his eye, the others still burning inside.

Everything felt so weak... he just needed to sit for a moment and think...

"I don't care what your swords aren't afraid of!" he yelled nonsensically, his voice suddenly echoing out into the mountains. Wendell raised the dagger, his hand almost shaking, and prepared himself for the pain of being cut to pieces. But it was true - he didn't care anymore.

"I don't care what your bones aren't afraid of!" he howled irately. "I don't care what you think you're not afraid of!"

He shivered with furious misery, and gave a spiteful snort. Without thinking he stooped over, grabbed a pebble, and hurled it down at them, pointlessly.

It clinked off a shield and went tumbling down the slope. A dastardly grin slowly formed on Wendell's face. He had held off whole fields of ravens once... all by himself. He had pigeon-holed crows thirty feet away as they flew. He had chased away a horde of ravenous blackbirds with a handful of gravel.

Now he picked up a larger stone and threw it down the slope. It slipped between a skeleton's shield and armor, and the spine crunched and crackled in half. Wendell gave a hilarious laugh.

He skipped up on one foot, sending another stone whirling down, down, down to the front rank. It smashed open an empty grin, sending the skeleton toppling backwards onto its friends.

Wendell stepped into a kind of dance now, scooping up a rock and leaping to throw it, and all the while the laughing and taunting them. Now he clapped his hands together, threw another, and leaped forward on one foot, defying them to make it the few feet up to him.

He laughed at their rusty swords and their stupid ninny grins and their shaky armor, until he found the words becoming a song, and throwing at the end of every line:

"Sticks and stones will break your bones,

but swords will never hurt me!

"What good to keep those swords so sharp,

while aim does not desert me?"

"Whether skeleton or not, no better than a birdy!

better go to bed and rot, for my name is Curdy!"

And other nonsensical nonsense as he could come up with at the moment. Soon skeletons struggled in vain to ward off the deadly rain. If they covered their faces, he smashed their feet. If they covered their legs, he smashed their arms apart. If they tried to make a way through piles of their broken comrades, all the while Wendell sent missile after missile hurling, swiftly evading their shields and swords. Broken arms and legs twitched across the ground, trying to climb.

Slowly he made his way backwards up the switchback, all the while stopping to send a few more rocks to the chaos down below. Finally, almost crawling up to the door, he was surprised that he had hung the key around his neck without thinking.

Wendell quickly turned the key. The latch opened with a bright click, and he paused for half a moment, trying to see if the wolf was still there... but then he went quickly through and shut the door tightly.

Through the door, the sky was all of a sudden bright and blue. He was standing atop a grassy hill, blowing in a wistful breeze. Looking down, there were neatly arranged hedges and a path between them, something like in the castle gardens.

26

Wendell didn't know how long he had been on the hill. He woke up to find himself staring at a startling blue sky, and for a moment he forgot where he was. It was so pleasantly warm here. There was always a gentle, gentle breeze that never changed.

Looking down from the hill, there was a little valley with hedges, and a path between all the greenery. It did look like a maze after all, but not even a very difficult one. It wasn't that large at all!

Wendell looked carefully, trying to see if anyone was there, but he couldn't tell. He was very sorry to have left the wolf behind, but there was nothing to do about it. At least if this was the maze, it shouldn't take very long to get through, he thought hopefully.

Soon the friendly winding path led to a wider space with a stone well on one side. Strangely there was no bucket but the whole well was filled to the brim. It was made of rough gray stones piled in a circle. He hurried and dipped a finger in the water, looking down a long, long ways into a kind of hollow emptiness.

The water tasted salty but somehow delicious, like the flavor of a forgotten memory. He almost recognized it from somewhere, but couldn't remember where.

"Tear-water!" he muttered. "I think. But why?"

Once inside the maze it was taking a lot longer than he had expected to reach the other side. Now he went around a bend, and there was another water well there just like the one before.

Wendell halted completely and looked at everything carefully. Did he make a wrong turn, and end up right back where he started? He got out a copper coin and put it on the well's edge. He made sure to take a different turn than before.

The well was there again. And again he went by, and the coin was still there, on the rock where he had left it.

There was another place, with a willow tree sitting on a grassy hillock. It looked as ordinary as everything else.

It was beginning to get lonesome, even though the greenery was so fresh and cool around him. He wished that at least the wolf was still with him. It was like the maze outside was making a maze in his head, as if he was now trapped in his own ludicrous thoughts. There was no one else to ask, for once!

Even though it made absolutely no sense, Wendell decided he should take the path that went past the willow tree, instead of the gray well. It was the only thing he could think of to do.

But suddenly, the tree wasn't there anymore, no matter where he looked.

"This is impossible!" Wendell snipped to himself. "I've passed that willow tree a dozen times. Why can't this maze make any sense?"

Then he slumped against the side of the path. Think, he thought. Right about now, Garim would always pipe up and say something like, "To give up is to fall down." He laughed heartlessly at the stupid joke. Surely Garim was very wise, but what good would that advice do in a meaningless, nonsense place like this?

He decided to get up for one last time. Hey, maybe that weird old guy was on to something! After all, he knew a lot more than Wendell, probably!

It must be near somewhere!! He heard Garim's voice urging him onward. "Remember, quitters never get anywhere! At least if you keep going, you'll get somewhere!" Just a few more steps... just a few more more... a few more...

Wendell really didn't know how long he had been walking. The well was mocking him, with his endlessly stupid hope and forceful cheerfulness.

If only there were skeletons to fight, more rivers to cross, something, anything but this horrible nothing place! If someone left clues for him why didn't they just show up? How did he know there was anyone helping him?

Finally, he hung his head. Okay, he thought, I'll do it. I'll keep walking, whoever you are, and I'll keep going until you show me the way, or I go crazy. Wendell gave a great, terrible, endless sigh. He didn't feel better at all, but he knew what he was doing at last. The maze of his mind straightened into neat rows, even if they were rows that were never got anywhere.

27

He passed by the same place innumerable times. Karen would never even know that he kept looking for her forever... he smiled a bitter, defiant smile at the thought of her finding out, at least. He was exhausted now beyond all feeling, but he held himself up straight as a soldier now and walked towards the next turn. The willow tree was there. And there was something under it.

Something bluish. And pudgy. And very very silly. It was laughing and laughing, and when the thing saw Wendell it had a lot to say.

"What took you so long? I've been expecting you all morning! Hee hee ha ha ha! Of course, you're not the only one I've been expecting... but the others weren't as smart as you. Not for a long, long time. Ha ha Hee hee!"

"What? Is Karen here?"

The blue thing tilted its head rakishly and smiled.

"Is that what you fear? Oh, dear!"

Then it burst into a mad fit of giggling, the likes of which Wendell had never seen. The thought of Karen trying to figure out how to get out of this place was not a funny thought to him.

"Tell me where she is!"

"Is that what you will miss?"

"Why don't you be quiet?"

"I never thought to try it! Hee hee!!"

Wendell's fingers dug into his hands, but he made himself quickly calm down and think... this thing... creature... liked to rhyme. Maybe he could trick it into saying something useful!! It stopped laughing, and starting rocking, back and forth, back and forth, humming a little tune. Wendell almost found himself swaying too.

"I have a secret I won't tell, I won't tell, I won't tell..." the tune went as it sang.

Perhaps something rhyming with east, if that was the way to go next...

"Did you get so fat at a feast?" Wendell asked cheerfully, in time to the tune.

"I suppose, to say the least!"

"Was the food the very best?"

"Better than the rest! Hah ha!"

"Did you stuff it in your mouth?"

"Why don't you ask Mrs. Bouth?"

"Did you then try to go forth?"

"That's what it was worth, Hah ha!!"

Then the creature went back to humming and rocking, rocking and humming. There was one more thing to try.

"You have a secret you won't tell, you won't tell, you won't tell?" Wendell asked innocently.

"Well, well, well, you've said it well, I have a secret I won't tell!!"

Wendell thought for a moment, a sly grin creeping onto his face.

"You smell..."

The creature stopped rocking and grinned back at Wendell, mischievously.

"Very well, very well. I smell very well!!"

Wendell danced a little fierce jig and grinned even more.

"Do I go forth?" he sang.

"No, you don't go north," The beast sang, dancing too, and grinning.

"Do I go to my best?" he sang, snapping one finger and turning to one side.

"No, you don't go west."

"Do I go to a feast?" he sang, calming down a bit and beginning to feel a bit happily anxious, until he could hardly bear it.

"No, you don't go east."

The thing was waiting.

"Do I go... to ... Mrs. Blouth?" Wendell asked finally, trembling, even though he already knew the answer.

"Yes," the beast asserted, nodding and smiling with satisfaction, "I tell you with my mouth, you go South."

Go South from the well... Wendell thought about it. He had always passed it going North!

The well was easy to find now, and Wendell walked up to it, and promptly turned around to go back the way he came, to the South. But now the maze had changed to a single pathway, going off into the distance...

28

Wendell woke up, leaning against the side of a hedge. He must have stopped to rest while walking down the long, straight path, and fallen asleep! Wearily, he got up.

There were some leafy trees hanging over the hedge wall now and then, hanging with bright apples or lemons or oranges, and he stopped and tried to cut some down with the sword, jumping up and slashing at the high branches, but only succeeded in gathering some smashed remains.

But it was very nice to taste something so fresh and juicy, and the stupor of the maze was quickly forgotten. The sun moved in the sky again, and Wendell hurried along at a good pace now, easily forgetting about his sore feet and aching limbs.

The sky began darkening tremendously, and stars glistened out of the twilight, sending a cool chill across the land. Suddenly he realized that the path was gone. He had been walking through a grove of fruit trees for some time, it seemed.

The trees grew taller and taller now and more entwined, until he almost had to feel his way along through the pitchy darkness, full of unseen tree trunks and ground that crunched into the silence all around. Wendell wished that soon he could find a way through to wherever it was he was going, he didn't even know.

He had heard many stories about such forests, of course, about the horrible things that were supposed to live there, but there was nothing but dead silence around, as if the forest stretched on with unmoving trees forever.

Now a patch of soft light appeared ahead, and he stepped around a tree trunk and looked out into a clearing, more of a huge dirty hole than anything else. And then there was a great, great tree, sitting on a small hill in the middle of a lake of dark morass. Great, stolid branches spread out from a behemoth trunk, frozen in timeless growth. But many of them sank down again, dipping into the fetid pool below, as if reaching for something. The branches all curved about as if trying to form an elegant design, but never quite reaching far enough.

Wendell felt a prick of sadness as he looked at the great tree, as if he saw an undying tragedy. But, he told himself, it is only a tree after all, and can't actually feel anything. He snuck past it sorrowfully, almost looking back to say he was sorry he couldn't help.

Slosh, slosh, he went through the muddy lake. Why was this place so dreary? It couldn't have always been that way, could it have? Wendell tried to imagine it as a bright, happy place, but couldn't find any clue of how it would have been, no stunted green tufts even, nothing but endless dirt and ooze.

He remembered there was a minstrel's song about a beautiful forest, someplace called Alehren, a long time ago. But even if there was grass and everything here, it would still look rather ordinary like any other clearing he had seen. In the stories, dreary places always sounded adventurous, but this one was just an empty mud hole.

Something was moving. Wendell looked back at the tree, but it was always the same, stuck in motionless misery. The sound was somewhere ahead, almost like the wind, but deeper. First a rushing noise, then a grumbly whiffling, over and over again, back and forth. But Wendell continued on.

There was a steep rise ahead, featureless, and he was relieved that nothing was up there. Coming closer, he saw it - another door, similar to the one he had found before... slowly he crept towards it, the sound becoming much louder. It must be the wind whistling through some cracks!!

He stopped, suddenly. There was something right there, perhaps an old, fallen tree in the shadow of the slope, and he had almost stepped on its root. Straining with his eyes, Wendell tried to form a shape from the shadows. Now the rushing noise went through, much louder now that he was so close. How very strange!

There was also a bump, and the trunk was somewhat curved, and... Wendell stiffened up into a statue and took a sharp breath. It wasn't a tree at all. A huge, sleekly black dragon lay curled up underneath the door, breathing peacefully. At least it looked like one; it was hard to see in the shadows...

The wind shivered through Wendell's feet, making him feel a bit unsteady, and after a long time of staring at the bump of an eyelid, he took a small, small backwards step. He strained his eyes again, trying to force himself to see something else, in the dim light. Perhaps it really was an odd tree trunk; after all, it was so dark! Yes, he thought, squinting one eye open, it does actually look like a tree after all, doesn't it!!

"What a dunce I am!!" Wendell thought, snickering. Then the tree seemed to stir a bit. The ground smushed under his foot, sounding loudly in his ears. Now he slowly eased his other foot off the ground and turned, turned around, stepping each foot now so gently at a time.

By the time he had gone back to the lake, he couldn't see the dragon anymore, not that far away. Perhaps he really had just imagined it. Surely it would have woken up, would have smelled him, if it really was...

He sloshed through the waist deep muck around the tree, not sure of whether he was feeling tree roots or some kind of slithering as he passed. Finally, he rested against the trunk of the tree, and felt his breath finally slow down again. Now he rested his head and closed his eyes.

A bit of wind brushed his face, and then again... he looked about, and one of the branches was swaying idly in the breeze. If only this great tree could walk, he thought, then it could surely pick up the dragon. Now the branch seemed to lift up out of the muck a little, and then some more... then the end lifted out. Wendell jumped up on his feet and grabbed the hilt of the dagger, waiting. The branch seemed to kind of mope about, and then finally sloshed back into the mud. Wendell took his hand off of the hilt and watched again, but nothing happened.

After a while, he had almost convinced himself that he hadn't seen it. Perhaps it was a stronger wind than before that had done it, a sudden gust. But what if the tree did know what it was doing, why did it just give up?

He thought for a long time, looking up at the great, defeated branches. If only there was some way he could ask it something, but he didn't know how to begin. If I was the tree, what would I be thinking, Wendell asked himself, staring up into the faceless form of the trunk. Perhaps it had lost something in the mud, and was trying to find it again... but how could I know that was truly what was going on, he thought?

It was at times like this that he felt the loss of his companions most keenly. Garim would know something, or the soldier would have some ideas, Wendell thought bitterly. But there was no one to ask, no one anywhere, except a tree that couldn't hear him or say anything. A tree that needed help but couldn't tell him what was wrong.

Somehow, as he thought of it, it seemed strange to Wendell that he had gone this far without any help, even though that was what he had set out to do. He didn't even know how he had found his way so far into the maze already, except by random luck. But he couldn't think about that now, he had to try and help the tree.

Going down into the muck a tiny bit, Wendell fished around with his hand, feeling some squishy things that he quickly let go of. The tree lifted up a branch ahead of him, almost warily, and then paused. Wendell looked at it.

Then the branch went up higher and unfurled in the direction of the black sleeper, gesturing pointedly. Wendell felt himself growing cold. The dragon? What did the tree want? Perhaps the dragon had eaten something, and Wendell would have to kill it and rip its stomach open... a sharp, icy feeling shivered over him at the thought of waking it... Perhaps he could kill it in one strike, right through its thick skull, but he didn't think so. Not hardly. A queasiness went through him now.

Wendell stepped closer, right up to the tail of the "dragon", and looked carefully at it. There was something he had missed before, a necklace around its large neck, dragging on the ground, holding a large amulet with a vile, strange symbol on it. He petrified into place, standing up straight now, breathing stiffly. It was alive, whatever it was. He got down closer and saw rows of scales now, more clearly.

The black dragon gurgled in its sleep, and Wendell started backwards, almost tripping. He needed to get away. Now. Even a wolf could be fought, but not this! Dragons were thousands of years old, and knew everything, and were stronger than steel!! And here was one, sleeping in front of him, and if it woke up and saw him then... Wendell shook his head desperately, clearing his mind. No no no!! He couldn't leave now!! Maybe there was another way around... somewhere... He looked down again at the powerful form, and seethed in his breathe, closing his eyes tightly...

The door was right there behind... if he jumped onto it, maybe he could open and get through before... no!! It would wake up sometime, he had to just try something. Anything. But then he would be dead, of course. If only this dragon wasn't... this stupid dragon...

In a fit of outrage he drew the dagger and poised it above the black skin, then froze before it struck. Those scales were harder than steel, surely!! In every story, he heard of how Curdie had faced dragons, and imagined him so sure and brave, sticking his sword into their sides with a mighty swing. But if he did and it woke up then...

He made himself stop and try to think; how did he even get this far, if he was just going to fail now? There must be someone helping me, a far-off wizard was watching him, or a ghost or something else even... but he didn't feel anything different than ever. Perhaps Garim said something about dragons. He always said that you should stab a dragon through the heart. It seemed like the stupidest way now, and he didn't even know where the heart would be!! No, this isn't helping!

"Are you still with me?" he whispered without even a hint of breath, but there was no response at all, not even a tiny whiff of breeze. But he couldn't just give up now, after going so far!! But he needed a plan. Carefully, he turned and went back through the muck and walked behind the tree. If only the tree could hear him, they could plan something!

But then a smaller tree branch lifted up slowly, out of the muck. It wandered closer to Wendell, and he stood waiting. The branch dropped something by his foot. It was a stone, kind of large. The tree pointed its branch behind itself.

Peering around the edge of the tree, he saw the dragon, sleeping in the shade. It was far away, but he could do it... he sent it flying, then quickly ducked behind the tree again. A howl went through the air, and Wendell quickly went about to the far side of the tree trunk, waiting and hiding.

Something spoke inside him, something sibilant and vengeful, as if speaking through walls of clenching teeth.

"You think you're clever, don't you."

Wendell didn't move an inch.

"You think perhaps you're hiding well."

There was a limping rumble of steps, coming closer, and splashes of water.

"We know where you're going."

The splashes grew louder. The voice grew smaller but darker.

"But we don't care."

A swarm of water flooded across the dirt.

"We're not at all afraid - of orphans."

All the tree's branches writhed into motion, and Wendell heard thrashing and squealing. He looked up in amazement as the dragon's black weight was thrown into the sky, and many branches were poking and prodding at it as it fought furiously to break free. Now a branch snapped suddenly, and the dragon fell all the way into the great black lake, twisting and roaring with torching fire. With striking speed it splashed about and leaped at Wendell, but the tree's branches had already swooped over and caught it again, cradling it up into the sky. Something dropped into the lake.

Now the dragon wrestled free and dropped into the lake again, roiling furiously. But the tree held its ground, branches spurting out into a forest of spines, and the dragon turned and limped away quickly into the forest.

The tree sent uncountable branches diving down, down, deep into the muddy waters, and finally brought up the amulet, hanging on a broken chain. It crushed and crunched it with its powerful boughs, until there was nothing left.

Wendell watched now as the tree spread its branches proudly up into the sky and froze, although everything was still as gloomy as before, and there was nothing more to see. Wendell stood watching and wondering for a long time, before turning to find the door again.

This door was much like the other one he had seen, only with no keyhole. But the designs were much different - somber, less flighty, and they hung on the door with great weight. Wendell almost thought he knew what they meant, but couldn't tell himself anything about it, other than he wished to go quickly through and not have to hear what they were telling him anymore, things dreadfully wonderful, that frightened him with their beauty.

But he forced the door open and stepped through. Only there was nothing "through" except black space. He felt along for a while, pulling himself along the small emptiness, until reaching another door, which he pressed open on hands and knees. Through the opening portal, fresh air whistled in, and he looked out onto a wide, high hilltop, with wild rushing grass growing everywhere. Then, after he had crawled out, he finally collapsed.

29

Wendell stood and looked down from a hill. It was hard for him to comprehend anything he saw. A huge, unending labyrinth stretched out far below - stone walls twisting and sneaking around deviously, defying his eyes to make any sense out of it. They went on endlessly for ages, a mindless ancient trap.

He tried fervently in his mind to follow a path somewhere, again and again, but there were too many ways, too many winding turns, too much to remember, that he couldn't hold it in. It was like the green hedge maze was just a child's joke, made only to taunt those who found the true maze.

A wind brushed past his ears, first this way and then that, making all the grass tumble and flow about. There was no noise here, except the wind. Wendell knew he was terribly, utterly alone here, where no one had ever been since unknown times.

Of course, he would need to go down and find an entrance somewhere. He only knew that once he was inside, there would be no finding the way back again.

He stood and stared into the distance now at the intricate pathways, trying to think of any way he could get through it, some way to climb the walls perhaps!! But there were so many walls, that it might be quicker to just walk. Think, Wendell!

But as usual, no one was there to tell him anything, and no thoughts were found by his searching mind. If only he still had the wolf here at least, that good faithful wolf!! The wolf had been a good friend to him, a good guide, even though he thought it was an enemy. Wendell felt a meager comfort at the memory, at least.

If only he had such a friend now! It would make all the anxiety and desperation less, even if they didn't know how to do anything either.

Do anything, do something, do everything... the words were familiar, and Wendell wondered where he had heard them before. They sounded so important for some reason.

"I always succeed at whatever I do."

It was the riddle, perhaps, that Garim had spoken so long ago... what was the rest of it? But the words sent a shiver through Wendell nonetheless. He had passed through so much already, and he didn't even know how!

Maybe the... riddle's answer had helped him somehow! Whatever it was called. It gave Wendell a strange feeling, to think perhaps he hadn't been alone all the time; but even so, that nameless one did absolutely nothing to show they were listening, or could hear his puzzled thoughts about them.

If only they would show up, say something, give him a sign to let him know!! It was maddening. But if they didn't show themselves, why were they even bothering to help at all? What purpose could it serve? How could he believe in what he didn't even feel?

The wind swirled about Wendell now, but then died down, an ordinary breeze as always. In the stories, the heroes always succeeded, but Wendell couldn't remember now how they did it. It was like a hazy memory as the labyrinth sat before him, never shifting.

Finally, he made his way down the hill, trying not to fall over and roll as it became steeper and steeper. Then the ground all began to level out, and the walls were higher and closer. He stepped across some more rocky ground, and walked between one of several high arches in the outermost wall that he could see, and the corridor stretched on for a long, long ways before turning. Wendell looked up at the bright green hill, and then stared into the unyielding stones. He tried very hard not to remember how the maze had looked from up there. The path led now ahead, and then left and right...

There were some small scraggly trees growing along the way sometimes, with apples and lemons, and Wendell gratefully cut into the juicy flesh with his dagger. At least he wouldn't have to be concerned about starving away!!

The obvious problem of finding a way through hung around him always, a deadly veil. If he kept walking and walking, like he had in the smaller maze, he really would go around in circles this time, and there was no willow tree, no blue monster to tell riddles here.

He still thought sometimes of Garim's own riddle and what it might mean, just as on the night when he had first heard it. There was something about a wall, and a fire that couldn't go out, and a child finding something...

He didn't know whether anyone was there with him, or anything. But even so he still caught himself saying something to them every now and then, rambling on about what he was planning, and about why they didn't reveal anything now that he needed it most.

Left, straight, left, right, around, straight, right, left. The paths made no sense. He could tell that he was getting somewhere, but not in the least where that somewhere might be. Finally, it was night, and he collapsed against a wall and lay asleep.

30

Early in the morning, he woke up. At least it felt like early in the morning. The shadow of the stone walls was long, with everything silent as a tomb, except for distant wind somewhere above. The stones were so cold and burdensome against his back. He got up now, and tried to wake himself and get warmer, pacing up and back across the small stretch of wall where he had fallen asleep.

Picking a stray, fat blade of grass now, Wendell gathered some dew from crevices in the wall and sopped it into his mouth over and over.

"Which way did I go last?" he said to no one or nothing. He suddenly realized he didn't remember which way he was going before he fell asleep the night before. Wendell wanted to bash his stupid head against something; he should have left a marker for himself!! Now he could end up backtracking all of his progress. The sound of a bird came from the early morning sky, and he looked up. It was the first moving thing he had seen anywhere.

A small hawk was flying slowly, a little ways off. The bird's cry sounded again, and Wendell hurriedly realized that it was not a small bird. It let out a long rising shriek, and Wendell quickly flattened himself against a wall, so that it could not see him as it flew by. The shriek suddenly became louder, until the whole sky quivered ravenously. It let out another fierce cry, and a gloomy darkness banished the faint sun as it passed by.

Then the shrieks died away, and Wendell slowly inched himself away from the wall and looked into the sky, before ducking back again. It was gone, at least as much as he could tell for now.

Wendell made his way along with greater caution, always checking the sky for dark specks or moving shapes. Another great avian flew overhead once, but it never noticed him, and he wondered where they were even going, or if they were looking for him, or even cared. He asked the invisible one, pleading earnestly that they should give him an answer, but no one responded, and so he felt worse than ever. Perhaps there really had been no one there.

Sometimes he sang the old songs again, quietly, just to have something to think about. He finally could tell his direction by the shadows on the walls, and the time of day, but he didn't know if there was an exit or even if this whole thing got anywhere! Perhaps Karen was simply lost inside, just like he was now.

He thought of shouting something and listening for a reply, but then birds would surely hear him.

The endless idea to ask his nameless helper came to him again and again, uselessly, but that was so stupid. Even if Ren Zael, the ancient warrior was watching, or Curdie's ghost was somehow there, surely they could do something to let Wendell know! Even if it was a small thing.

"My words they are always the same..."

Wendell continued the old songs, trying to remember where he was in the vastness of the passages. After a while, all the turns blended together and lost meaning. It was a frightening task, and despite the sun's warmth he felt a chill iciness growing inside. He fought to convince himself that he wasn't already lost!

"If you can't hear me, don't fear...

I am still near, am still near...."

He kept singing the old hymns, in a hushed way. They gave him a meager comfort, as he sang the notes, which were full of a calm hopefulness and mystery. So calm and so hopeful, as if they were written in a place where terrible mazes and lost girls didn't need to exist, a world far away from this awful, endless tomb.

Then Wendell listened to his own voice.

"If you can't hear me, don't fear...

I am still near, am still near..."

But this song was written hundreds of years ago, he reasoned. Anyone could sing it anytime, anywhere they wanted, and it would be the same dumb words, he knew very well. What was next though?

"My words will be with you, all days,

my words they will guide you always..."

The lilting tune went up and down, back and forth, sometimes breaking forth joyously, sometimes subdued and hushed.

"Listen to what I have said,

my words they are always the same,

my words, are your meat and your bread,

my words they will guide you always..."

The tune kept on, going about playfully.

"When you know that I am near,

then you have nothing to fear,

My words they will show you the way,

my words they will guide you always..."

The song ended, as it always had, but not with a final note. It was more like a question mark. As if the tune was waiting for something more... but what came next? Where was the rest of the song?

Wendell turned a corner now. If the writer's words were always the same no matter what, who could be helped by hearing them? The author didn't know what Wendell needed, when he wrote the words down so very long ago!

"If you can't hear me, don't fear...

I am still near, am still near...," he sang again, the melody going about joyfully.

He stopped suddenly, feeling a bit strange at his own words. That would be an answer, at least. Finally, an answer to something, to anything!

Who even wrote this hymn though? How could they be near? It still didn't make a tiny bit of sense!! But Wendell hummed the tune anyways, and the words danced about, just like they had... with that big blue monster thing that liked to rhyme... he got to the end of the song, and heard the questioning last note... the song wanted an answer, a reply! It wanted him to answer the question!!

Wendell spoke up, trying to rhyme his own ending to the song now.

"You are still near, are still near,

even when nothing I hear!!

Now what would rhyme?

"Even when you seem so far,

I will still know where you are!!

Even when nothing I hear,

I will still know you are near!!"

The song rose so triumphantly and finally ended, full of certainty and confidence. Wendell stopped again and waited, looking around, waiting for something to happen, anything.

There was no reply, no genies appeared from the wall's cracks, no magic beasts appeared to fly him across. But he didn't even need a reply!! At least the song told him so...

"You are still near, are still near..." Wendell sang as he pushed himself down the pathway.

31

Wendell hurried quickly that day and the next, and all the miserable uncertainty that followed him for so long gave way at times to a bright vision of hope. Just suppose that someone was with him, and had helped him along the whole way! It was a thought he clung to with desperation as he passed through small, winding corridors, towering high with grey stone.

Sometimes one of the large birds would circle him, high above the walls, and he would have to run from one wall to the next to keep out of sight. But then they would be gone.

Wendell tried asking for directions, but there was no answer... still he never passed the same place twice, as far as he could remember.

In the loneliness of grey stones and distant sky, the memory of the painting was always a fading ache in his mind, and sometimes he almost found himself asking Karen where he was, as if she could hear him, and wondering what he would say if he suddenly found her somewhere past the next corner.

Still he wandered and fled for a wasted eternity. The path turned a bit, and then suddenly opened up wider. A long, thin courtyard sat ahead, looking greater and more impressive than anywhere else.

It was walled in with large grey stones like the rest of the maze, although these were smoother and better shaped. There was nothing else to show what this place was here for, no traces of banners or decorations, or even a pillar.

For some reason Wendell knew this had been an important meeting hall once, he didn't know why. There was something in the look of the stones, a kind of feeling or nobleness that he couldn't begin to understand.

Wendell found himself walking more carefully here. As if he himself was now royalty, simply by being in the ruins of what had once been.

Looking at a far end, there was a giant, ancient brass plate hung up for all to see. Two enormous doorways awaited, one at the left wall, and the other at the right wall.

That's strange, he thought. Who would put up a message in the middle of this maze, where no one would possibly ever read it? Going quickly up to it now, he reached up to brush off some of the rust and read carefully.

"Traveler, you came this far,

no longer knowing where you are.

It matters not, how you came,

just find your way back out again!

'Look from the sky for the way you should go,

then look to the sky, and the way you will always know.' "

Well, I should check where the doorways lead to, and then come back, he thought eagerly. It was simple enough.

He took the left path, and immediately it was a dead end. Wendell turned and went back. Well, of course he should take the right path then! It was the only way. Quickly he hurried back past the hanging plate and went along... it was a dead end as well!

How could he look down from the sky? If both ways went nowhere, then why did some ancient ruler decide to put up this plaque in the first place? How...?

Wendell smothered the need to be exasperated. Whenever there was a riddle before, it had an answer. He just needed to wait, listen, and be reasonable. Right.

Maybe he could ride one of the giant birds! But the birds may not even have been around, when this plaque was first bright and new. Who knows how long it has been.

Even so, he waited and waited for one of them. Finally, he heard the bloodthirsty wails again, but wisely decided to find another way.

The walls weren't that smooth, but after a bit of tussling with the hard stones and a few nasty falls, he gave up trying to climb them.

Look from the sky... it was probably something obvious and stupid as usual. He just had to do it. Okay, fine. I'll look from the sky, you old ancient rulers! Why not?

Wendell laughed at the idiocy of the thought. He closed his eyes. So I'm up in the sky... there's me! Heh heh... and a long, wide corridor, and two dead ends on either side, turning back and.... well... I'm standing in a huge arrow! It must point the way! But once I leave this hall, how can I even know where to go?

"Look to the sky, and the way you will always know..." he read again.

He looked up right above the metal plate, and there was a high, far away mountain peak sticking up above the wall, marking the direction. He just needed to keep it in sight, and he would know which turns to take!

Feeling very trembly and excited, he went back down the corridor, and tried to pace himself as he went through the labyrinth again, always checking the mountaintop for which way to go.

32

It was getting darker and chilly, and Wendell almost wished to just stop for the night. But up ahead there was an opening! Tears came to Wendell as he saw the whole mountain clearly now. He got up now and hurried along, almost running out of the confining walls.

At last he was outside in the open again!! The wide, beautiful open!! Which was getting very dark and cloudy. But in the morning it would look better of course. There were a few trees ahead... he went through them, excitedly, pushing onward through the branches. The ground sloped down for a short while, and then he came to the other side of the thicket.

He sat and rested for a while, looking down. There was something way down below, scrunched into the foot of the mountain, with an old, old river before it. It was hard for Wendell to tell what he was seeing in the dim light.

Whatever it was it didn't seem to have any lights glowing inside, but it had endless towers and buttresses that mixed into with the mountain's shadows. The place was surely abandoned after the maze had been built, just like the meeting hall had been.

He woke up, but it was night now, and there was no point in trying to go back to sleep again. Wendell began stepping across the scraggly dirt of the long, long slope, watching the wide, starless sky above for any sound or wings. There was still a bit of frigid, seeping wind.

It was taking quite a while to walk down the slope because he had to walk back and forth to keep from sliding too much. It was hard work, and soon he longed to reach the river and get a drink.

Looking at the castle now, it seemed to have no features in front, no carvings or decorations or anything, nothing to rest his eyes on, just mindless empty walls.

Nothing, but a single drawbridge closed in front of the wide river, taller than any house Wendell had ever seen, hanging with chains and metalwork. Quickly he hurried along until he reached the river's edge.

By then he knew that he could not possibly reach the water. It was too far below, and once he had jumped down, it would be more than difficult to find a way back up.

Wendell stood shivering and watching the empty windows. The river went past with a loud murmuring below, but there was no other noise. Now a sharp clink echoed into the air. Wendell looked about.

There was another clink, and then another, then faster and faster. Sounds of massive chains and machinery grinted and ground, the drawbridge shuddering downwards. Wendell froze with hesitation, then in a sudden fit leaped down all the way to the water below, and felt the icyness close over his head.

His eyes were closed, and he stretched out furious hands against the rush of water, trying to swim back up before the water choked him. He reached the surface and gasped, looking up over the top of the moat. The drawbridge was already halfway down, but inside he couldn't see anything.

Quickly, he strained over to the side of the sluggish river side and pulled himself under the drawbridge's shadow. The clammy stones of the moat's wall gave his desperate fingers a few handholds as he pulled himself up now, right under the falling drawbridge as it shuddered into the dust.

Now Wendell reached up and snatched the dangling chains, holding himself into as small a space as possible, his heart working furiously, feet pressed against the wall. He tried again and again to hold in his breathe, but still it came out with great violent gasps. Something began pounding on the enormous drawbridge.

Hundreds of hooves shook the immense wood, but then very suddenly it stopped, and there was no noise left to hear but things racing off into the distance.

He hung there for a long time, listening to the muddled trickles below. Pain slashed his fingers and toes, but he didn't budge. A clink shuddered through the drawbridge. Then another. The grinding began again. Wendell was left to listen helplessly as he was pulled up and hung in the air, his fingers crying out for relief from the sharp edges of the chain. Finally, it stopped, and he found a place to rest his foot on the side of a great bar wrapped around the drawbridge's edge.

Looking up from the bottom of the bridge, he could see the top of the first parapet above. He looked down at the river below. It looked cozy and inviting now, more than the empty air around him. He scrambled as quickly as possible up the side of the drawbridge, flinging his arms up to the next chains each time, his feet digging helplessly against the rough wood, until he reached the top, which was splintered and cracked.

Then, with a tremendous heave, he pushed up from the wood to a crumbled spot in the wall, and with another panicked shove, he put one knee between a crumbled spacing. It was still a ways to the top of the wall, and there was no way to jump down again.

Wendell hung from the wall, resting his forehead against the flat stone, and closed his eyes with weariness. Now what? He looked up at the top of the wall, soaring ludicrously into the sky above him. How far away, he could not tell.

There was nothing he could do now, he had nothing with him to help him climb, unless he learned how to fly before something saw him there. Except his dagger, and that was no help at all!

"Please... " he pleaded into the stale air, trying to reach out with his mind and find someone to help him. The song said they were there, even if they never answered aloud. If they helped him before, they would do it again, of course.

"Please, you must lift me over, " Wendell continued, hopefully. Surely if they were there, if they couldn't speak back, at least they would hear him, and do something!!

"It's very important, " he went on, hearing his own words, whispered into the stone. "I just need a little help. Just once."

"Why don't you ever speak?" Wendell muttered angrily. "Can't you see I need some help!?"

But the cold stones didn't reply, and his fingers were beginning to hurt against them. He looked down at the black waters below, judging the distance from the corner of his eye. He would never survive the drop.

"Is anyone listening?" he said pointlessly.

Wendell hung his head down against the wall, his arms beginning to tremble with the chill and terrible weariness. Tears of frustration stung in his eye, and he grimaced against the wailing fear below him.

"Why don't you do something?!?!" he sobbed. But who could he blame? He had climbed the wall alone, and he would break his silly neck alone.

Now the struggle to keep his fingers dug into the crack became desperate, and he felt his foot sliding down. Angrily he kicked and struggled to hold on, all the while feeling more miserable and filthy from the weeks of useless traveling.

"Please... I'll do anything you want..." he whimpered...

But there wasn't a reply even still. But there must be!! Any moment he would find himself soaring in the air, just like in every good story. What where they waiting for? What did they want? What did they want from him?

Wendell hung his head one last time to think, terror clouding his every dizzy thought. How could he know. He knew because. But it could be coincidence. Always coincidence!! And now on the wall. If they did something, he would know!! If they said so, he would know!!

"Maybe we are being clear and simple," Garim's smug voice replied in his mind, automatically. Then Garim smiled.

"To those who listen, I listen," he rambled on randomly.

Wendell fought the urge to howl and hurl himself down into the water. He was so miserable. As soon as he touched the water, it would all end... peace at last... but instead of peace, Wendell felt only a bottomless, dirty feeling at the thought of dying. He would not be the only one to die.

He gritted up a final desperate thought to his hollow mind. "To those who listen, I listen." I will listen, he thought desperately into the air, hardly able to feel his arms anymore.

I will listen.

He looked down at the river, and saw it, past his sword's hilt. Perhaps...

With one hand, holding on excruciatingly with the other fingers, he drew the dagger and struck wildly at the mortar above.

A corner crumbled with age, and Wendell gave a start of glee. He pushed the dagger's tip into the crumbled cracks, and pushed himself up, the pain in his fingers forgotten. Now he continued up the wall, and finally heaved himself onto the parapet.

His fingers cramped with endless numbness, and he nursed them in his mouth, trying to understand what had just happened. But he knew inside that he didn't have to ask! That was what they had wanted from him all along.

On the other side of the wide parapet was an expansive courtyard, emptier than anything Wendell had ever seen. There were no weeds growing between the cracks, no stray bits of crumbled stone lying in the corners. It was only square and vacant, paved with fitted stones that stretched from one end to the other, in dull shades of blue misery.

He clambered down the chains and machinery of the drawbridge now, seeing that nothing was there, and quickly went across the long ways towards an empty, black doorway. For some reason he wanted to creep along one of the walls instead of going down the middle, but there was no use in that, he told himself sharply.

He listened carefully by the doorway, straining his ears for anything in the darkness, but couldn't hear anything at all.

"Go with me now," he said boldly to the listless air, staring into the blank opening, a smug smile creeping unbidden onto his face. Wendell stepped into the frigid portal, holding the dagger out before him.

33

Something smelled horrible and dingy, like meat that had rotted for a hundred years. Wendell held his nose with one hand and swung into the darkness with the dagger, trying to feel if anything was there. It was absolutely black, and he wasn't sure there was even any floor anywhere. After a while a bit of light shone up ahead.

He crept along carefully, carefully, and saw that it was a measly torch, hanging on a wall. Three pitiful halls stretched away from the light with nothing beyond them.

He paused for a long time by the torch, which flickered sometimes from the cold but never burned down. He couldn't just stand there forever he knew, but there was no difference between the pathways, nothing to show him if one went to a treasure room and the other fell to a pit.

Finally he had an idea. He took a small pouch he had taken along and shook out some coppers and brassies. Then, carefully, he stepped down the left-side way and threw a small coin ahead into the empty space. It was silent for a long while. Then a faint splash echoed, and he quickly went to the other hallway and threw another coin. It clinked a few times and was quiet. A deep growl shuddered through the stones, but then there was no more noise. The little torch flickered again and kept burning, but nothing else happened.

There was only one hallway left, and quickly he chose a brass coin and threw it ahead. The tinny clink of metal on stone echoed a few times, and then stopped. He tiptoed down that way, careful not to make too much noise.

Soon he came to a little rotted door and bashed it open with the dagger. A few glittering candles met his eyes, shining off of boxes and piles of treasures. It was more than anyone could carry away, but there was no point in dragging such stuff along now, and he didn't bother to think of how much anything was worth. But he quickly found some pouches of round, small gemstones and put them on his belt, and then went out through a small door on the other side, peering through first.

Black iron walls bent up to an empty ceiling, rigid and featureless. There were no alcoves to hide in here, nothing but endless chambers of openness. Now he waited behind the blank corner of the massive passageway.

The floor began rattling, and with a pang he realized that of course this place was not as empty as he could hope! But what would be large enough to cause such shaking? Perhaps there were huge machines here, with some horrible task, or some part of the castle might be falling apart, after so many years. He glanced around the corner in a quick way, and there was a huge, towering shape nearby, going along slowly. Wendell stopped looking and shrunk by the wall without a sound.

It was a frightening thing to see a living giant, even though he had seen the paintings before. But he had never understood the huge, brutish weight and searching eyes that had inspired many travelers to terror and wide-eyed stories, only to be laughed at by others. He understood their terror now, but he couldn't let it rule him! If only he tried he could trick it, just like he had done before with so may other things… like Curdie would do…

Quickly, without arguing with himself Wendell took out two large emeralds and poised one up high. It will be no different at all than chasing crows, he assured his thoughts as he aimed carefully at a spot far away.

But there was no time left to think, or to feel afraid as the floor shook more and more terribly. With a snap he threw, as he had so many times before, and the emerald soared up high and dashed onto the stone floor with a ring.

"One raven," he muttered to himself as he spurted out from the corner and threw another gem behind the giant's back. Now Wendell changed direction and headed for another corner. The emerald struck against a wall, clanging loudly.

"Two ravens," he said to himself encouragingly. Now the giant turned about, startled, but Wendell held a large diamond already. As the great foot lifted up, Wendell skipped the diamond across the floor with precision, just as the giant stepped.

"Three ravens," Wendell murmured, as the huge monster stumbled back wildly and smashed into a wall. Now the flailing body crashed downwards, dazed from the fall, and the enormous hall shuddered and was suddenly still.

Wendell sputtered over to the side of the fallen monster. A filthy smock, belt, and enormous boots, covered the giant as it lay sprawled on the ground. Wendell still shuddered as he looked at the unconscious face, but he moved closer and closer to see if there was something useful he could quickly borrow. He noticed something promising, a large ring of keys dangling from its belt, some larger than his own hand. He ran over and reached up to unfasten them. They fit snugly around his belt, next to the dagger, and he hurried away without looking back even once.

Traveling through the empty, towering halls, he could hear more giants stomping in the distance. Gratefully, there was a small door carved into a corner, and after trying several keys he went through. He had to leave the key ring behind though, because it rattled much, but he promised himself that if he needed it he might return.

He found himself on a rampart now. He had gone up a winding, ancient stairwell that went on for some time, and then opened at last to the sky. The rampart overlooked much of the fortress, and a stale wind tried to press him back against the old stones. A single thin tower rose high above the rest not far away, where a torchlight flickered in a small window. That must be where Karen is being kept, he thought suddenly for no reason. It could be the easiest place to guard he reasoned, and she could hardly run away.

Even though it might not be true, he had a terrible, lonely feeling about it. She was there now, just a crow's flight away, he thought. Stuck right there, where he could see but never reach. His eyes hurt too much from watching the window and he went over to the rampart's edge, covering his face against the thrashing wind.

He looked over to see if there was any way down and across, but the wall slanted backwards after a few feet down and there was no way to climb at all! If only he had some rope of some kind, a very long rope!

But if he could remember always which direction the tower was, he could make his way along the castle's passages... until he reached it! And then if he could climb up, and then get past the guards and cut the chain and then... it was a lousy plan, but that didn't really matter to him here, watching the window. Wendell took note of distant mountains, and then went through a different door than he had come from.

The walls here were shorter, slimy and reeked of foulness. If he was going to make this ridiculous idea work, he would have to find windows sometime and see his direction every now and then, he thought hurriedly while scurrying down one way and another. There was a door here at the end, but it was locked good and tight! It was a solid door, and would bear much battering unfortunately. Even the keys he had taken might never fit. But then the lock rattled, and something, someone was coming through.

Wendell ran back down the passage again as fast as he knew how. The sound of hinges followed him, and an ugly speaking between two voices was heard.

There was a sort of dining room on one side of the hallway, and he shut the door behind him after going inside. If they passed by this place, he could sneak around and get through without being caught! Wendell waited, listening very closely for a long time. Footsteps echoed carelessly closer and closer, and the talking went on. Then it all stopped, outside the room.

Wendell looked around, and saw a table decked with a rotting tablecloth, and flung himself under it. The door wrenched open thoughtlessly. Soon two boots stuck under the tablecloth as an orcish creature sat down at the table and began a grisly feasting on something.

Crackling bones and gorging went on above Wendell on the tablecloth. He slowly crawled away from the creature's feet, and peered out from the cloth at the other end. There was some kind of cabinet there, with its drawers and doors shut tightly, but it might be helpful!

Wendell remembered now a story about Curdie, and he had an idea. Although he knew that people always feared orcs and ogres, the orcs also feared people, and were not brave at heart. But if he was going to do this, he needed to do it right!

Quickly he took his dagger and prodded the cabinet with the tip, rattling one of the drawers, and then snuck away to the other end of the table. The sounds of feasting stopped quickly and there was a snort of disbelief. The orc got up and muttered blackly while going over to the cabinet, and rattled the drawers for itself.

Wendell looked up through a crack in the table, and could see where a pitcher was. He shoved the sword's tip up and tipped it over, spilling a dark liquid with a crash. The orc gave a cry of alarm and rushed back, but Wendell had already gone to the other end and was rattling the cabinet again. Then he rushed back across the way, and went out from under the tablecloth and behind a shadowy tapestry hanging in one corner. As the orc looked at the cabinet stupidly, Wendell whispered, "Curdie... Curdie..."

The orc spun around then, and ran from the room. Giving up the ruse now, Wendell rushed out back to the hallway and followed the retreating footsteps, not too closely but always just behind. The door that had been locked tightly before was hanging wide open, and Wendell went through after watching to see if it was safe.

An ogrish bellow of pain came from somewhere in the distance, and some more strange words. Wendell hurried along now, sometimes hiding in dark prison cells that were along the way, as more orcish denizens ran past, some fitted with crude armor. Then he would sneak out again, and press forward.

There was a winding, curving staircase up ahead, and he realized it must be the tower! Wendell drew the dagger and stormed up, not bothering to see what was ahead. The many steps turned around and around and around, and then he was there at the top, but there was no one there except a few empty chains and a pile of straw. After looking around for a few desperate moments, he had no choice but to hurry down the steps again.

34

After a long while, he lost all direction in the ludicrous floors of the castle and sat to rest, in a forgotten chamber with black iron walls. He lay for a while on the hard stone, even passing in and out of sleep a number of times. But he couldn't stay there forever, or even let himself sleep for too long.

He still had to foray out into the castle to search eventually of course, and only a dismal determination kept him from huddling in a dark corner somewhere. At times there were creatures to sneak past, ogres and bats and watchful goblins, and at other times the walls seemed to be the only friends and enemies for hours on end, as passages led nowhere and to nothing.

Sometimes he peered now around an iron wall before stepping out into an open hallway, or slipped through a tiny door with a key filched at great risk. Once he had left a safe place behind, he knew he would never be able to find it again, but had to keep moving farther along to stay hidden, even if for only another moment.

Many times the faint light of torches and tiny windows gave way to total blackness, and Wendell had to feel his way along the walls of small, wretched places that twisted through the castle, around and around and up and down.

Over the next hours or days, he couldn't tell which, Wendell felt that the place was not built out of stone or iron, but out of withering fear that seeped into his skin and howled in the empty walls.

Soon, the game of hide and seek became desperate, but Wendell felt a growing defiance of the rules, hitting goblins from behind with gemstones even as he whispered plans to an unknown ally, then ducking under horrid black staircases and tables, now stepping out brashly to lock another door, the keys swindled with his dagger from the belt of an ogre, after sneaking up behind it.

He needed to rest sometimes; but often there seemed to be no catty-corner that was left to hide in, no room without two doors and a dark tunnel beside it. The deeper he went, the stranger and more cunning the inhabitants became, until the halls were a dismal wasteland of waiting danger.

Wendell stepped through them boldly all the same, now even throwing bits of a taunt song down the hall behind him, as he outwitted another monster of its precious keys.

"Halls to find me are halls to hide me,

you'll never find me,

I've got the key!!

Halls to show me, are my way-to-go-ee,

you're left behind me,

I've got the key!!"

At last he found himself in an abandoned room, far in the castle. It was raining outside a small window, high up in the wall, and he put his hand out gratefully to catch the raindrops as they blew in. The water felt good on his dry tongue.

An amiable, lispy voice spoke up.

"It is trying to hide. Nurmur knows it."

Wendell looked behind him, but stopped himself from shouting in fear. There were cracks and gaps in the wall, and the voice came through them clearly.

It continued speaking.

"Nurmur has seen them before, trying to hide from the ogres. Bad, bad ogres! Nurmur's mommy would not be happy with them."

Then another voice said something, this one a bit lower and somewhat stupid sounding, like a character named "Doofus" Wendell had seen at the puppeteer's tent during the village festival.

"Murnur has seen them too, trying to hide. Murnur tried to help them, but they ran away. Murnur was sad."

Then the other voice lisped again.

"It is afraid of us, Murnur. It thinks we are going to eat it. Nurmur doesn't like stringy meat. Nurmur likes yummy marsh potatoes. Yum Yum. Nurmur steals them from the ogres. Naughty, naughty ogres!!"

The doofus one continued right after.

"Ogres don't know about the door under the stairs. Ogres will never find Nurmur and Murnur."

Wendell wasn't sure if he trusted Nurmur and Murnur, but he didn't have much of a choice at the moment. After looking behind a few doors, he saw a black staircase with a shadowy alcove underneath.

There was a tiny hatch there, completely invisible in the darkness... it groaned opened with a bit of a shove, and Wendell eased through, leaving it open for a moment to look around.

There was a long, long hallway, with many doorways, all of the same size but some without any door, and some with no rooms behind them, only a small blank space. After a while of stepping cautiously along, he made it to a staircase, which led up to another hallway that stretched on and on.

Wendell continued along, but then suddenly stopped. There was a sound of discussion in one of the doorways, but very different voices from Nurmur and Murnur.

35

Wendell paused outside the doorway in the long, endless hallway, listening. He heard voices, which seemed calm and unhurried. He tried very hard to hear what they were saying.

"...hasn't found him yet, of course."

Another voice spoke up, this one darker and yet fiery.

"...is listening outside in the hallway right now. Aren't you?"

Then they continued talking, as always. Wendell shook his head. He must have heard wrong. If they knew he was there, why didn't they come capture him? He leaned a bit closer to the doorway.

"...would've known he would go looking for her, of all ones... isn't that right, Wendell?"

Wendell tensed backwards, his heart pounding ferociously. Perhaps one of their names was Wendell also. Oh, that must be it! He turned slowly to walk back down the hallway. Nothing happened.

"Don't be afraid, Wendell. We know you're here. Come in, please."

This time the voice was louder, more authoritative. Wendell froze and thought of running, but there was no point now. He slowly stepped to the open doorway.

There was a room, very well-lit compared to the rest of the castle, with a fireplace and some very ornate chairs around it. The walls had beautiful decorations on them, insignias and tapestries with interesting, lovely designs on them. There seemed to be a calm silence to the room.

"That's it. Come in, the fire is warm! We've been expecting you, of course."

Wendell slowly stepped into the room, and looked at the speaker. It was what looked like a very tall, tall man, resting in a large chair.

He had a very regal, pale face, and long, black locks flowed down past his ears. He was wearing a peculiar set of clothes, with lace at the edges, and the air around him seemed to seethe with a strange, wonderful beauty.

He turned his head a bit as Wendell entered, and fixed him with a dignified, respectful stare. The other one turned in his chair to look at Wendell also. This one Wendell wasn't sure was human, but something close. He also was tall, and almost smoldered with hidden strength. The first one spoke again.

"You don't have to be afraid of us, Wendell. We're not trying to hurt you. See?"

He held up his hands in a gesture of helplessness, and then brought them back down unhurriedly onto the arms of the chair, all the while still resting in it. Wendell opened his mouth to speak, but nothing came out.

"Poor child," he said, laughing.

"He thinks we're trying to stop him," he muttered to the other.

"He doesn't know, if he wanted to come here, all he had to do was stay in one place. We've been looking all over for him, haven't we?"

The other one nodded, seriously.

"You see, we know you. Do you know who you are?"

Wendell looked at them, confusion swirling in his mind.

"You are the perfect one. The brave and true! So is Karen. We brought you here to be together, to fulfill your destiny. You are the rulers of the world."

Wendell looked down and tried to think. What if it was true? What if they had been looking all over? A great sense of relief and happiness came over him. Karen was okay! These must have be the ones who left clues for him, and guided him through everything!!

He heard the first one speak again, smiling happily.

"We brought you here to teach you deep magic. To show you the secrets of the world!"

Wendell looked up at him, still feeling tremulous. The man smiled a small, joyful smile.

"All your dreams are about to come true, Wendell."

Wendell's heart was still racing a little, and he wasn't sure exactly whether he should say something or do something. Slowly he started to put his dagger back, which he realized he was still holding.

"Don't listen."

Wendell looked to the side to see who was whispering, but no one was there. The first man looked at him puzzledly, and a flash of consternation went across his face, but then was gone.

"Do you hear anything?" the first one asked.

Wendell looked at the man's eyes, which looked back, searching him, serious and full of concern. He was sure they could hear his heart racing, and he wondered why he didn't just tell them something immediately.

Even so, he thought he recognized the voice from somewhere, but he couldn't remember where, even though he tried so hard to. It wasn't Garim, or anyone else... but it was so familiar, it made him hurt somehow to remember it again, as he stood hesitating, the two men watching him intently.

Finally, he said something.

"No, I thought I heard something, but I guess I didn't."

Why did I say that, Wendell thought.

"That's good," said the first one again. "No one but you should hear what we have to say. But first, I have something for you Wendell," he said, smiling brightly.

The second one reached inside his jerkin and pulled out a small perfect stone, a brilliant blue. He held it with two fingers, as if he was afraid it might scorch him.

"Come, see for yourself. It's very rare... in fact, there's only one like it, but red... you know to whom that belongs..."

Wendell came a bit closer, his heart still pounding unmercifully. He reached out for the stone, and as he came closer to it, it seemed as if all his worries vanished away, and he felt happier than he ever had in his life.

But he felt also that if he touched it, he could never go back to... to what? What could be left behind?

"Don't touch it!!"

A harsh whisper sounded in his ear, and he jerked his hand back, startled. The feeling of elation dissolved, and he felt

again as if he recognized the one who spoke to him. Could it be...
the wolf? No, the wolf had never spoken.

But as soon as he remembered its great, fierce eyes, the
memory burned inside him. It did remind him of the wolf, but it
wasn't entirely the same.

Now he tried desperately to hide his confusion from the
two men, who glanced at each other gravely. But didn't they send
the wolf to help him?

"What is wrong?" the first one asked, seriously. "Is
something wrong?"

Wendell didn't know what to say. He slowly reached his
hand for the stone, and felt the happiness again... as if he could
do anything in the world... he was the perfect one... nothing
would be wrong again... but then the memory of the wolf's eyes
came, and he jerked his hand back again, defeated.

"I... I can't. I don't know why."

The two men looked back at him calmly, sadly.

"This is more serious than I thought. Let us bring Karen in."

36

Wendell looked around suddenly. It was her! As she walked into the room, it was as if a wind of fiery perfume rushed through. There, on a necklace around her neck, was a red stone, just like the blue one. She smiled a nice, happy smile.

"Well, Wendell, what are you waiting for?" she said, smirking. "There are so many things to be done."

Wendell looked back at the blue stone, sitting so round and elegant in the man's palm. All he had to do was take it. He reached his hand out again, his heart hammering terribly as it got closer and closer, the feeling of happiness coming back stronger this time... there was no reason not to.

But somewhere inside, behind the happiness, he felt a twinge of loneliness and desolation, and without thinking he took his hand away again. Karen started to cry.

"You don't love me after all..."

She buried her face in her hands and sobbed uncontrollably.

"I knew it was true... but I didn't want to believe it..."

And her sobs became choked and miserable. The two men looked at Wendell, confused. Suddenly, for some reason, Wendell thought of something.

"Um, Karen," he began very gently, not even knowing why he was saying it, "in the painting of you... why were you smiling? I... always wanted to know. If you tell me, I'll take the stone."

She looked up suddenly, startled, a vague, puzzled look on her face. Then she smiled, wiping away a tear.

"Oh, is that all? I was thinking of my mother, the queen. She was so beautiful, you know. That's all."

The answer rang hollowly in Wendell's ears as she spoke on. It seemed as she spoke that it wasn't such a big thing after all, and he felt disappointed. He thought it was some precious secret she had. He was sure of it!! But it wasn't.

Wendell turned to look at the stone again. It sparkled brightly and was filled with a deep, wonderful color. But somehow he couldn't shake the nonchalance of her answer. Now everyone was looking at him, and he reached for the stone again. Somewhere inside, he thought desperately back to the painting... to her smile, so bright and full of laughter.

It couldn't be!! It had been so long since he had seen it, perhaps it was only her mother after all. He closed his eyes and forced his hand onward, trembling with consternation at himself.

He pressed his eyes shut even tighter, and felt the warm glow of happiness, closer and closer... suddenly he stopped.

No. Karen was lying. They made her lie! He knew it. What was he doing? She would start crying again. He just needed to take the stone, and everything would be okay. He closed his eyes more and more, but the memory of her smile wouldn't go away. At last, he dropped his hand. He knew inside that the answer was a lie.

"What have you done with Karen?" he demanded suddenly, surprised at the loudness of his own words in the room. The two men looked at him with honest bafflement.

"She... she's right there, Wendell."

Karen looked at him sweetly now, although tears were forming in her eyes again.

"You can't tell that it's me...?" she said miserably, her eyes pleading gently with him.

Wendell felt a familiar feeling of despair rising up inside, one he had felt so many times before, and it seemed to burn away the calm quietness of the room.

"Where is she?!?!" he shouted now, reaching for his dagger quickly. What am I doing, Wendell thought hesitantly...

The first man looked at Wendell questioningly for a moment, and suddenly his face changed, becoming fierce and commanding.

"You don't know what you're doing. These things have been planned for thousands of years!!"

Wendell drew his dagger quickly and brandished it before him.

"I don't care! Tell me the truth!!" he demanded.

The first man stepped up out of his chair, and took a step towards him, looking at once taller and deeply powerful. The second one did nothing. Wendell held the dagger up.

"Tell me where she is, or else I'll cut you both down!!" he said.

"Do you think *you* could defeat us?" the man replied darkly, stepping fearlessly towards Wendell's raised weapon.

Now the second man raised himself from his chair, muttering a fervent, howling chant. The muttering grew louder, and Wendell realized it was music, a music that was terrible and black.

The tapestries on the wall fluttered, and a wind swirled into the room, brushing against him softly.

But then the wind stirred up into a maelstrom, until the fire was dying out. A strange, deadly feeling surrounded Wendell, and bitter fears hid everywhere. He tried to concentrate, but couldn't even begin.

He needed to get away, but there was nowhere to run to! Danger was everywhere, behind the chair, out in the halls, even under the floor...

Wendell opened his mouth now and tried to scream, but couldn't. He was shivering now, and wanted to find a corner and die. He dropped on his hands and knees, the dagger clattering to the floor, and tried slowly to get away to the doorway. The men moved quickly to block his path, and he was trapped. Miserably, he crept towards the chairs, but there was no way.

"Sing!"

The whisper came again, urgent and encouraging. Wendell opened his mouth a bit, as if afraid that the darkness of the room would creep in, and began to sing with all his might, a fierce whisper, something lively and rousing and strong. Now his voice grew louder, and the others raised their voices forcefully, trying to weave notes of deception into the pure, brave hymn. But Wendell kept on, feeling the song pour out from inside him.

The wind in the room whistled louder... no, it was another voice, a fourth voice, joined with his, ringing with the purity of gold.

"...songs in the night, to break through the fright,

songs in the night, to keep you.

Sing in the night, of the glorious light

and your song will light your heart...

For without eyes you'll see,

and without fear believe,

when the light is in your song...

Sing in the night, of the glorious light,

and your song will be your dawn..."

The dark men's voices faltered lamely, and the lingering promises of misery and fear suddenly were hollow and worthless, until Wendell laughed inside that he had ever been afraid of them in the first place.

The fire blazed up again, and Wendell grasped his sword and ran at them, but suddenly the room was nothing but a hollow chamber like all the rest, cold and empty.

37

Wendell went out of the room, but now a thin hallway stretched before him, emptying into the darkness. Endless small black doors lined it, each one silent and the same. Wendell stepped down the hall now, listening carefully.

Was something whispering? It was hard to know. Perhaps it was just a cold feeling swirling about him.

He thought about opening one of the doors, but they didn't have handles or markings, so he continued on and on, trying to never look behind.

Now Wendell stopped. A single black door lay open on the right side, as the rest watched grimly. There was no light behind. He peered into the darkness, and kept one hand on the dagger's hilt. There was nothing, nothing he could see inside.

Perhaps he should keep going, and there would be something at the end of the hall! But he forced himself to edge into the doorway, feeling ahead with the drawn dagger.

The black was everywhere, and lingered in the air, old and rotted. Wendell tried turning about to find the doorway again, quickly, but couldn't. He spun about again. Where was he? He tried stepping briefly ahead, but took his foot back quickly again. Then he remembered, and began a song, something he heard many years ago, but was suddenly new in his memories...

"...darkness, hiding only fear,

a black veil to hide the tears...

a veil so you will never find

a treasure that was left behind..."

"...darkness is a sleep of death,

hiding what your heart wants most.

So that you will never know,

never know that it was there…"

"…darkness is your only fear,

a black veil to hide the tears…

a veil so you won't go and find

a treasure that was left behind…"

Now Wendell pushed forward, stepping in time to the rhythm, and soon the dagger clunked on something he couldn't see. Quickly he reached and wrenched a door open, and a meager, wretched light came through.

Now he wandered through desolate hallways again, that never seemed to lead anywhere, although he went up and down many narrow, rigid staircases.

But he had a sense that he was going down more than up, although he still didn't know where he was. Sometimes there was a window, high up in the wall, but he still couldn't tell if it was day or night. The darkness of the rooms was thick with the strange, horrid smell of fear, and Wendell wondered how anything could survive in such a place.

Sometimes it seemed as if someone had just been in a room as soon as he entered, and once or twice he was sure he saw someone disappear around a corner, as if they were following him in a backwards sort of way.

He could never go fast enough to catch them, or it, and so he paid little attention.

Now he leaned around a corner, looking. It had been a long, long time since any ogres had been seen, but he was still as cautious as ever.

Something flitted out of view, a bit of ragged cloak or something. Quickly he ran after them now, throwing away all caution, but they ran faster as well, opening a small, black door now leading to a wide, brighter passage.

"Wait!" he yelled softly, but still they wouldn't stop. Now they tripped and fell as they came into view, and turned around to look at him, and gave a high, terrified scream. It was a girl, with a destroyed white dress, and very dirty red hair. Her face was streaked with dusty tears and smudged with black, but as Wendell looked at her, he felt very odd somehow.

"Oh, you're just a boy!!" she laughed, looking very composed all of a sudden, all the terror gone out of her face. She tossed a bit of hair out of her eye, and looked at him very matter-of-factly. Then she got up quickly, and carefully brushed off the back of her dress, although it was a pointless act.

"Hallo. I'm Kimberly," she said almost carelessly, brushing aside the same bit of dirty hair again.

"What are you doing here?" she said now, rather straightforwardly.

Wendell thought she might be speaking a bit rudely, but she didn't seem to know it herself.

"I... I'm a prisoner," he said, not knowing why he was doing it.

"Good thing you found a sword," she said, pointing to his dagger, "I tried to steal one too. It was tricky though. The ogres aren't always stupid."

Wendell was rather disheartened to find out that it wasn't Karen after all. He supposed he would have to tell this strange girl the truth eventually, of course. But he knew that Karen couldn't possibly be so rude or stuck up as she seemed to be already! She did have red hair and all, but he couldn't imagine her to be the girl who was smiling so wonderfully in the painting, and her voice was hardly "wild and quiet" as the soldier had said about Karen!

Now she started walking down the hallway, as if expecting him to follow. He walked alongside her now, feeling very strange to be with this unknown girl.

"I don't suppose... you know any way out of here..."
Kimberly asked.

"Not really," was all he could say.

"I'm sorry I screamed," she said with a flippant sincerity,
"Half the castle must be looking for us now. Well, how did you
escape?"

"You first," Wendell said politely.

"It wasn't that hard," she said seriously. "The ogre was
leading me up to a tower, I knew, and I started talking to him
about his mother and being a good ogre, all the while pretending
to be afraid."

She went on, "Then, halfway up I bit his hand and kicked
him in the shin, and he was so surprised I ran away... I got away
easily."

Soon she was so absorbed in the story she forgot that it
was her question in the first place, and now they continued on in
silence.

"So where are you from?" she asked nonchalantly,
peering up ahead.

"I'm an orphan, from the royal city," he answered
truthfully.

"I'm from the royal city as well," she said.

Now they rested for a while, although there wasn't much
comfort in the cold, featureless room. After a while, they decided

to take turns setting out, and then retracing their steps, so as to make some sort of map on the floor with Wendell's sword.

She insisted that he go first. So Wendell went out through the left door (or was it the back door?) and explored for a while, very carefully trying to remember the path he took and avoiding any places that were too dark.

After a while he carefully, carefully went back, and was very relieved to find himself opening a door and seeing Kimberly sitting there, with her back to him. He stopped before saying anything.

"Oh, that's not what he would say, let's see..," she was saying to herself quietly. Then she looked around suddenly.

"Oh, it's you," she said, in her usual manner.

"You shouldn't be away so long," Kimberly continued, a bit snippishly, "After all, you took the sword with you. What if the ogres had come?"

"Alright, here, have the sword. It's your turn," Wendell said, trying to be polite. He took out the dagger and handed it to her as she got up.

"This is heavy," she said simply, straightening up a bit after first holding it. "Why do they always make these swords so heavy?"

But she held onto it nonetheless, and went off towards the front-hand door, going through it into the shadows beyond.

Minutes passed. Or were they hours? Wendell began to be a little anxious. What if she got lost? He almost decided to go through the next few doors, to make it easier to find her way back, but soon enough she appeared again.

"Here," she said, handing back the sword.

It seemed to Wendell that sometimes he saw her saying something to herself in a wistful voice, and giggling, when she was gone too long and he had to go looking for her, but she always just looked up at him as if nothing was wrong. Perhaps she recited poetry to not get bored or afraid.

If he left her alone for too long she would be rather angry with him, always saying that he had the sword and she didn't, and he thought that perhaps she could try to be a little nicer sometimes.

Soon there was a tidy map on the floor, scratched with the point of the sword, which seemed to make little sense or help.

Kimberly looked down at their efforts. Then she looked up at Wendell with a gloomy sort of look.

"I don't think we're ever going to get out," she said.

Over the next hour, Kimberly seemed to be quieter and more irritable than usual. If she had anything to say, she said it quickly and sadly. Wendell tried to cheer her up with stories of how he had survived on the streets, but she only said he was a nasty boy for doing such things; even so, it never seemed as though she meant to hurt his feelings.

38

There was a distant noise of feet and doors opening. Kimberly looked behind, her face suddenly flushed with fear, and they both ran out, and towards the end of a hallway. But more footsteps sounded from the other side as well.

Quickly Wendell opened a small door, the only one in the long hallway, and she went through. Now they both went through more doors and passageways, until Wendell realized she was gone. But he had to keep on going, there was no way back now!

He kept on for a while longer, but suddenly he felt a pang of regret. He realized that, although she was rather aloof and not always nice, he actually missed having Kimberly around, and he thought that perhaps he should go and find her, and not leave her to the ogres again. She was rather scrappy, and could come in useful in finding Karen, of course.

But there was no time now! He stopped. No, he couldn't just leave her to be locked up again in this terrible place! It felt so heartless somehow. Turning about, he drew the dagger and listened by a corner. There was a sound of frantic yelling, a girl's voice, and something bellowing with grunty pain.

Quickly Wendell ran down the hallway, and followed the distant rumble of footsteps now.

Eventually, after a lot of twists and turns, he found himself sneaking behind a procession of horrible kinds of ogres, always waiting one step behind them. He peered around the top of a small staircase, carved dangerously narrow out of the side of a wall, and watched. Even if he did catch up, what could he do about it?

Kimberly hadn't been the best of friends, but he felt a dismal indignation welling up inside anyhow. It must be horrid to be chained up in that tower, never to leave!

Without thinking, he ran up the last step and into the corridor, but the footsteps were gone. He realized now where he was, he was outside the hallway where the two strange men had been, but he didn't stop now. He sprinted up to the portal, and suddenly they were there again, sitting in their chairs.

39

The room was larger now, and seemed to have a balcony overlooking the edge of the castle. The first man smiled at him wickedly, and Wendell realized that Kimberly was asleep, her head lying in the man's lap, who stroked her hair gently.

"Wake up, Kimberly!!" Wendell shouted, and the man looked at him with frustration. Then his face became pleasant again, and he put one finger to his mouth.

"Quiet, please, she needs her sleep," he said gently.

Then the man took out a red stone from a pocket, and started to lift one of Kimberly's hands.

"You can't do that!" Wendell roared at him, leaping to his chair without thinking, the dagger raised. The man flinched back for a moment, then raised the stone up. Wendell's dagger crashed into it and bounced off, harmlessly, and Kimberly fell down onto the floor, never stirring. Now the man rose up, broiling with a dark power.

"You don't even know who we are! You could never know!" he said, smiling with anger. A black sword flashed out of the air and he brought it down at Wendell's head, who clashed the dagger up into the blow, and was thrown backwards. Now Wendell leaped up again.

"You have no idea what you fight against!!" the man thundered, flashing the black sword with all his might. But Wendell met it and turned it aside. How did I even do that, Wendell thought randomly.

He parried another blow, pushing it back, and then stepped forward, forcing the man to back off. Now forward, now back, Wendell slashed to one side recklessly, now leaping forward again, now clanging the man's sword out of the way.

"I don't care who I'm fighting against! Who cares?" Wendell howled into the man's frustrated countenance.

The other one rose from his chair, all pretense of goodness gone from his frame, and from the corner of his eye Wendell saw him raise two hands in a horrid gesture. But Wendell quickly leapt over to him and made a mad swing for his ribs. The man leaped quickly backwards and threw something invisible, and suddenly a dozen ravens flew at Wendell, their beaks open wide.

He fell down and covered his head, and suddenly they were gone. But the second man gave Wendell a great kick now, and he sprawled on the ground, clutching at his stomach. There was Kimberly, sleeping peacefully.

Wendell staggered up quickly now, still holding his side, and raised the dagger.

"By the swords of David, of Curdie, *I defy you!!*" he wheezed. They were laughing now. But Wendell felt strangely stronger, the more he spoke.

"*You don't know who you're fighting against! You don't even know!!*" Wendell said now, feeling the pain and fear drowning in an endless sea of fury, as if a terrible dragon was arising.

"*You don't even know what you're fighting against!!*"

Wendell leaped at the first man now, who mercilessly brought his sword out at him. But the man's strike was glanced aside, and Wendell advanced. From the edge of his eye he could see the second man approaching.

Suddenly, Wendell hurled himself forward, the dagger pushing against the great black sword, sending the great man sprawling onto the ground. Now he turned to confront the other man, who stopped suddenly and put one hand out in a striking gesture, and Wendell felt a sharp prick in his ribs.

The man beat at the air now, and it seemed as if a multitude of hands were buffeting him, evading his attempts to get away. Wendell flailed his sword now pointlessly after him, as he spun and shimmied out of reach.

The first man rose up now, glowering with fury, and Wendell saw him going over to where Kimberly lay... Wendell spun about now, as an invisible hand slapped his face. He began staggering over, step by step, but it was far... The man knelt down next to her. Wendell hunched over as something dug into his aching stomach, and fell on one knee.

"You won't..." he gasped now, and staggered around after the dancing one... there was a great chair beside him, and with a terrible cry Wendell seized it over his head and brought it hurtling down on the man as he tried to skip away, sprawling him into a wall.

Now Wendell jumped up on one foot and threw himself at the other, who raised the red stone defiantly, blocking the deadly strike.

But Wendell brought up his foot swiftly into his chest, and he fell, gasping for breath. Wendell leaped after him now, and plunged the dagger down, a horrid black substance oozing out of the man's body as it tore open and disappeared, the red stone rolling onto the ground.

Wendell spun around, and saw the other coming, a towering maelstrom of strength and motion. As he raised a hand, a rush of wind came into the air, and as he lowered his other, a wave of fire followed. But Wendell cut through them, standing behind his sword.

Now the man stepped up on his feet and clapped his hands up to the sky, and rays of piercing lightning came out, but Wendell put his sword across his eyes quickly, blocking it.

Now Wendell saw him glance at the sleeping girl, but pretended not to notice. As soon as the man started to step towards her, he hurled the dagger suddenly.

The man gave a snide grin and put out his hand, but the dagger struck true and he staggered backwards onto the ground, wailing shrilly in surprise.

Slowly the man raised his head and looked at him with amazement, before he withered away into the air, leaving a puddle of odious black.

Slowly, clutching his side again and wheezing heavily, Wendell went and knelt at the side of Kimberly, but everything had changed back into a cold, empty room. Wendell found the dagger lying in a corner, and put it wearily back on his belt. Then he picked up the sleeping body and carried it from the room.

40

Eventually, Kimberly began stirring, and Wendell put her down on the cold floor of one of the rooms. She looked up at him, a terrified, defiant look on her face, and then calmed down.

"Where are we?" she said weakly.

"I don't know," Wendell said.

"I had a horrible dream." she went on, "I was taken by the ogres again!!"

Wendell considered telling her what had just happened, but he truly didn't know if she would believe him. She sat up now on one hand, and looked at the blank walls. At least now they could go and find Karen, if nothing else, he thought.

But there was no time to think, because footsteps were coming again, hundreds of them, and rumbling shouts and clanking metal sounds. Kimberly hurried onto her feet and looked at Wendell.

Together, they rushed out of a random door, and down a long, long flight of stairs. Now they turned, and went down another, and it became darker and darker.

"Where are we going?" she said quickly.

"I don't know! I don't know!!" Wendell answered helplessly.

Soon there was almost no light, and they found themselves outside a great, steel-gilded door. It gave way to their pull, and they rushed inside and screeched it shut. There was no light anywhere.

Wendell felt his way along, and suddenly tripped over something hard. There was a clanking, and he put his hands out to catch himself on the ground. It was a chain!

Wendell felt along the ground, and the cold, heavy chain was fastened to a great bolt. With fumbling quickness he unfastened it.

"Are you there?" came a voice, a little scared but also with a bit of indignation in it.

"Yes, I found something," he answered.

Quickly, he took the chain in the darkness, and tied the door shut. It was large and very heavy, and would likely hold against much beating, Wendell thought. If only he knew where he was!

There was a sound of something dragging, off in the darkness. Wendell listened, but the noise was gone. Rasp, rasp.

The chain began clinking across the floor. Now the door rattled in protest, as if something was pulling on the chain. Wendell heard a high-pitched scream of fear, and stepped in front of Kimberly, holding up the dagger into the blackness.

The door rattled more and more, and began creaking in protest. Something was thrashing about, and soon the door cracked, sending meager light into the dungeon.

The chain smashed free, and something tremendous went crawling off into the shadows. There was no time to think. The whole dungeon began shaking and shaking; something was throwing itself against a wall, cracking through stone and mortar, and then a rushing sound of water was heard.

Wendell realized what was happening.

"Grab hold of the chain!!" he shouted. They rushed forward against the flow of water that was ankle deep now, and clung onto the flailing chain. Soon the water was waist deep, rushing backwards against them, but they were dragged forward and forward, now floating, choking in the waves that washed over them.

With a tremendous lurch, Wendell found himself spiraling through a sea of water, now pulled which way he couldn't tell, up, down, or sideways.

At last Wendell found himself bursting out of the river moat beside the castle, coughing and choking up water, climbing higher and higher into the air. Looking down, Kimberly was still there, her fingers clasped desperately around the links of the chain.

The wind was bitterly cold against his soaked clothes, and he gasped into the rushing air, forcing all breath out of him. A huge Wyvern pulled the chain behind itself, with silvery wings and a rainbow body shimmering above.

Now the Wyvern twisted and turned, as the chain flailed about behind it wildly, as land and sky flew beneath in a tremendous rush. Looking down, Wendell saw many places he had been before, soaring past.

Besides him, now under him, now above him, the endless labyrinth where he had wandered for so long, the black forest of the forsaken tree, the green hedge maze. It all seemed to pass by in a matter of minutes, and then the Wyvern slowly lowered its wings and lowered itself over a grassy hill.

Wendell rolled onto the ground as it hit him from below, and he saw Kimberly already lying there.

For a long while Wendell simply lay on the ground, too dizzy to even move. Eventually, he pushed himself up and looked around to where he was.

Then, before anything else could be done, the Wyvern lifted its wings. It rushed ahead over the edge of the hill and flew away again, hauling the great chain behind it, before Wendell even knew what was going to happen.

Kimberly sat up sorely and looked around with blank eyes. With all the water and wind, the dirt had been scoured out of her hair and face, and her hair shone deeply red again. She had many freckles, and Wendell thought he had seen her long ago, somewhere.

"It *is* you!" he said, amazedly.

"What?" she said wearily, looking over at him in a weary way.

"Karen!"

Kimberly gave a startled look, and then said, "I hate that name! How did you know my name?"

"The king put out a reward for you! Everyone knows your name!!" he said, feeling a bit excited and yet dismal.

She looked a bit surprised.

"How much is it?" she asked quickly.

"Ten horses worth of gold," Wendell said, hedgingly.

Kimberly looked a bit disappointed.

"I was never the favorite," she said bitterly.

"And, he also promised, that..." Wendell began.

She looked up curiously.

"If anyone found you, they could marry anyone in the royal family."

Kimberly laughed.

"You could say you found me," she said, chortling, "and then... well, you'll have to meet my sister - Violet!! It would serve her right!!" she said excitedly.

And she laughed more and more, not in a nice way. Then she got up, and dusted her dress off rather thoroughly.

"Where are we? Well at least we're out of that horrid place."

Wendell looked around. The surroundings were normal, trees and such, like much of the forest near the castle, but that was nowhere in sight. Together, they started down the hill, going southward at Wendell's advice, saying he knew more about the woods from being an orphan boy.

41

He looked over as she made her way down the slope. It was her after all, there was no doubt now. But she was so different! Where was her sad smile? Perhaps the painting really was the only time she ever truly smiled. It was all wrong.

She still doesn't know, Wendell thought glumly, watching as she went on ahead. I could choose another of those princesses, and she would never even know... What about one of the crazy yellow-haired ones? They were kind of nice.

Kimberly looked back at him.

"Where are we going?" she asked.

"I don't know yet," he said, almost truthfully.

Walking back through the forest now, he looked about for his friend, the wolf, but there wasn't one. They stopped for a while to rest. There was something rustling in the bushes, and Kimberly got up to go look.

A strange little forest creature came out, and she bent over and started talking to it in a nice voice. It was a round ball of fur, with two friendly eyes, and two feet like a bird's almost. It started jumping up and down, squealing excitedly.

"I think it wants us to follow it," she said, turning to Wendell.

"Maybe it's just hungry," he said dryly.

She shot him a withering look and went back to pampering the little forest creature.

"Have you seen... a wolf anywhere?" Wendell asked.

Kimberly glanced over at him strangely.

"It's my friend."

She shook her head and went back to talking to the little forest creature...

"No, we don't want a bad wolfy, to eat you, do we now, little snoogums..."

It went running off, then turned and looked at them, chattering in a quick, nonsensical voice and hopping about. Kimberly went over to it, and Wendell decided it would be pointless to argue.

They followed the forest creature for the rest of the day, and then stopped for the night. They sat at opposite trees in the thick woods, too tired to say anything for a while. The forest creature sat and dozed off.

"Are there really *wolves* here?" Karen said quickly.

Wendell nodded tiredly. He still wondered what had happened to his friend.

There was silence for a while.

"Maybe we should take turns staying awake," she said, hopefully.

"That's a good idea," he agreed. "I could let you have the sword when it's your turn."

"What if we both fall asleep?" she said.

"We could sit at the same tree and put the sword between us, so whoever wakes up first can have it, if a wolf came," he said, hedgingly.

"A royal princess never sits at the same tree with an orphan," she said darkly. "It wouldn't be proper."

"Okay," Wendell said wearily.

"What?? You'll just let the wolves eat me?" she said, infuriated.

Wendell opened his mouth, but no sound came out. Karen closed her eyes and hung her head on her shoulder. Wendell closed his eyes as well.

"I'm cold," he heard her say pitifully.

Wendell thought for a while before saying anything.

"What should I do about it?!" he asked helplessly.

"I don't know," she said, caustically. "You're the one who always camps like this."

"We could try gathering branches," he surmised. "It's too bad I don't have a cloak. That dress really isn't made for..."

"It's a very *nice* dress, you *stupid boy!!*" she said with sudden fury, and turned over quickly to go to sleep, putting one arm across her face.

Wendell listened for any more words for a while, and then fell asleep as well.

42

Eventually the forest creature led them to the same river he crossed before. The boat was still there. They both got in, and Wendell paddled across, struggling against the current's flow.

They clambered back up the way the wolf had led him and Garim down before, and set off into the woods, back towards the castle.

Soon night had almost fallen again, and they had to stop before all light was gone. Karen sat against a tree, cradling the little forest creature and stroking its fur. Wendell leaned wearily against an opposite tree.

Now she looked around, and then looked at him in her usual manner.

"I still wonder where we are," she said honestly.

"Don't worry," Wendell said tiredly, "the castle is probably only a day away."

Wendell slowly realized that it had been weeks since he had seen another person, and he had grown so used to being alone with his own thoughts, it seemed strange to have someone else around, especially someone like Karen.

But he was still glad someone was there, rather than no one, just like when she first showed up in the fortress. Even if she didn't seem that excited that he was there as well.

The next morning, Wendell woke up, but Kimberly wasn't there. He looked around, startled, but no one was visible.

Quickly he got up, and tried to keep a dismal panic away. What if…?

There was something rustling in the bushes. Karen came through, looking distraught.

"Oh, I can't find it!!" she said miserably.

"What?" Wendell asked quickly.

"That little animal! It must have left while I was asleep!!" she said, distraught.

Wendell gave her a look of disbelief.

"How could you do this to me? You can't just leave before I wake up!"

Karen looked up, indignant.

"Why not? You have a sword!!"

"Don't you understand? I thought you were gone!!"

"I wouldn't leave you to wander through this forest by yourself!! What kind of girl do you think I am?" she said, outraged.

"I thought they captured you again!!" Wendell said, equally as loud.

Karen looked at him, understanding dawning on her face.

"Oh. Why didn't you say that?" she said, in an infuriatingly practical voice. But Wendell didn't feel like saying anything more.

Now they found some wild berries, rather sour, and ate as many as they could without getting a stomach ache. Wendell thought of telling her about the wolf and the rabbit, but then he remembered everything else he hadn't told yet, and wasn't sure exactly how to bring it up, and wasn't sure she would like to hear about it anyways.

Soon they set out walking, and Wendell tried telling some of Garim's stories about the candlemaker and the well and the other things, but somehow they didn't sound as nice when he told them, and soon he gave up.

"That's a nice story," Karen always said, looking off at the woods. The woods were much different now that there was no real hurry to get anywhere, and they seemed like such a calm and ordinary place now, full of mossy tree stumps and critters.

43

It took some persuading but Wendell finally convinced Karen to go into the watery tunnel, the one he had crawled through long before. He kept saying it was a forest shortcut he knew about. Shivering and miserable, at last they leaped out into the icy water pool, and a flood of distant memories went over Wendell, full of all the despair and hope he had carried for so long.

"Why couldn't we just go around," Karen snipped with disbelief, trembling with chill.

Wendell looked at her, standing and shivering. When he knew that she was only Kimberly, he had fought with the two men to help her. He had missed her then, when she was gone, even though she was mostly rude to him, but now he didn't anymore simply because her name was different. Why was it any different now that she was Karen again?

"What?" she said, puzzled, looking at his thoughtful stare.

Wordlessly, he turned and began walking back down to the forest clearing, down to the red flowers, to the forest path. Karen went as well, subdued and quiet.

It was Garim!! Wendell saw him, in the distance on a horse, and raised a hand of greeting, and the old storyteller raised one as well, jubilantly. Soon Garim reached them, and before he could say anything in congratulations, Wendell gave him a pointed look, and the old man nodded gravely, and gave a kick to his horse, sending it into a slow walk.

"Who's your friend?" Karen asked unconcernedly.

"Garim," Wendell said simply. "It's not far to the castle from here."

Karen didn't seem as happy as he had expected her to, even if she wasn't sad.

Once they reached a street of the city, one of the town guardsmen saw them and gave a shout of surprise.

"The king's daughter!!"

And he ran off into the crowd. The three of them continued, Garim's horse slowly walking through the street, and soon a battalion came to escort them safely. As they went onward, people realized what was happening and cheered for them, throwing little bits of things and hats into the air.

It was a bright, bright day, and the walk seemed to last forever, with the endless smiling faces of the townspeople, and villagers looking at them from every side. Karen seemed very used to it, and didn't even care much. Wendell looked in the crowd for Derrick and Collin, but never could find them.

At last they went up the royal avenue, and the pang of the memories brought tears to Wendell's eyes now, he heard his young, naive voice challenging the guards again, saw himself sitting among the trees, saw himself running to the king...

Now the bridge was crossed. Two rows of soldiers stood in motionless salute on either side. The portals swung open, and they stepped through the royal palace, sunlight streaming through openings high in the walls.

The two guards uncrossed their spears with great haste as they recognized Karen, and the whole procession went in before the king.

He was still sitting on his throne, leaning, looking ahead with a look that Wendell would never forget, so anxious. When the king finally saw them, he rushed down, down the steps, and threw his arms about Karen, and blubbered with great, raw, heaving sobs.

"My Karen... my songbird... my Karen..." he said, on and on. When at last his tears were spent, he turned to Wendell with a look almost ravenous.

"Anything of mine is yours, boy," he said fiercely, blubbering again, and patting him forcefully on the back. "Anything of mine!!"

44

Sitting back in his castle room, Wendell's thoughts were surreal. Now that all the excitement of his journey was over, he realized that he had no idea what he was supposed to do with the rest of his life. As an orphan, he had just tried to survive it, but now that seemed like a strange, distant memory.

It seemed strange to sit and try to remember everything that had just happened... but there was no time to rest now, there was a pounding knock on the door, and he went to answer it.

"The king summons you to the royal throneroom," the servant boy said, fearfully.

Wendell left his dagger behind and was led along, back to the royal chamber. There were five daughters he had seen in the paintings, the calm, rosy one, the one with wild black hair, the two yellow-haired twins, and Karen. There were also some other girls he didn't know, looking a bit confused.

A shout was heard from somewhere, "Violet! You come out here this moment! *Do you hear me Violet?*"

Then, a moment later, Violet came in, looking very indignant, escorted forcefully by two guards. She took her place and gave Wendell a terrible look.

Now the king came in, looking very pleased, as if he had just gotten an excellent price for selling some cattle.

"Which one do you choose?" he said to Wendell, who suddenly felt very much out of place. Wendell walked up to Karen, who was looking a bit out of sorts, then turned and walked down the line of princesses. Violet looked down her nose at him fearfully, consigned to her fate.

Tulip, one of the yellow-haired twins, giggled as he went past, and Lily, the other one, gave him a nice, polite smile. The older ones didn't seem very happy. Then he turned and slowly walked back, and then back again.

Every time he reached Karen, he was about to speak, but suddenly couldn't say anything. At last, he came back down the row and stood in front of her, thinking of what to say. She stood with her hands clasped together, and looked down at the ground. She looked up now suddenly.

"What?!?" she demanded.

"I choose you," he said, the words all rushing out now. "I chose you!! I did it all for you!!... I saw you in a painting then I snuck past the guards, I went through the labyrinth, I almost got eaten by dragons, I broke into the castle where they were keeping you..."

As he spoke on and on, a look of sudden awareness and hurt came into her face, more and more, and she shook her head, great tears springing into her eyes. Suddenly she turned and ran from the room, crying and weeping heartbreakingly.

45

Karen ran and ran, down the halls, through the gate, out to the gardens. What is wrong with you, she told herself. I don't know!! I don't know!!

Finally, she found it... her special tree, lost deep in the gardens. She sat under it, and thoughts came to her violently. Why would he do all that for me? She thought. Why would he risk his stupid neck just for me? Why why why?!? She cradled her head in one hand, and felt the tears flowing down her arm. I can't believe he did all that!! Who is that fool anyways?!? Why did he do it?? For me?? ...all the princes run away... I hate them anyways... I always did...

But there was nowhere left to hide from anything anymore, and princess Karen put her face in her hands, the tears shuddering through her like a knife.

46

"She has to come out eventually," the king said seriously, watching the gardens. "It will be night soon."

Wendell went back to his room and fell into a deep, weary sleep.

In the morning, he reached for his dagger as always, but was surprised to find himself in a goose-stuffed bed, back in the castle. Then everything came back to him. He had done it! Kimberly was okay. There was a knock on the door, and he went to open it. It was a breakfast tray.

He realized he had had nothing to eat for a long, long time, and suddenly hunger overpowered him at the smell of the food, and he felt very weak. After nibbling at a muffin, he felt a little better.

He came out of his room, and wandered down the hall. Violet was walking past. She turned and gave him a smug glance.

"I knew you wouldn't have the courage to choose me," she said coolly. "Now look what you're stuck with. A crazy girl who runs away from you."

Wendell's eyes burned with tears of hate, but he could think of no reply. She kept walking, and ran into a sitting room, laughing. Wendell suddenly turned and went into the sitting room as well, but she wasn't there. He turned to leave again.

Someone was walking behind him. Violet was coming back to taunt him some more! But this time he would have something to say to that sister, that...

"*Go away, you stupid...*" he screamed, spinning around.

Karen stood holding some beautiful white flowers. Just a moment before she had been smiling, just like in the painting, but it faded from her face, and tears of shame stung her eyes. She dropped the flowers and ran away, crying horribly. Wendell stood, unable to move for a long time. Then, slowly, he went to the flowers and picked them up carefully. The silly yellow-haired girl, Tulip, came humming through another door, then stopped suddenly.

"Where did you get those?" she asked amazedly.

"That's from Karen's special tree!! If I even touched one, she'd kill me!!" she said, fearfully.

Then Lily, the other twin, came through.

"Yes!! Don't let her find out, or she'll kick you for sure, you nice boy!!"

Wendell felt like saying something very rude, but for some reason he held his tongue.

47

Quickly Wendell went out through the door where Karen had left, but of course there was no sign of her. He couldn't see any servants to ask.

After wandering, he found the gate to the gardens. He went quickly from one place to another, but the garden was much more immense than he had ever imagined; there were more out of the way corners and courtyards than he thought imaginable.

It was a place of unending pathways, lined by beauty and mystery, as neatly laid out patterns of rose hedges gave way to places of solitude and wild, overgrown trees, and then led swiftly to rows of bright flowers. But there was no sign of Karen. He strained his ears into the soft breezes, but couldn't find any sound.

At last he found himself in a walled place of arches and corridors, some ancient, neglected meeting place. There was a faint noise from over one of the walls far off, but he couldn't tell if it was near. He kept on, wandering with an aimless desperation, never knowing what made him take one way or another.

Now there was a broken wall in some forsaken corner, and he stepped through, and went along a long, twisting, endless way.

After what felt like forever, the closed-in walls led to an empty courtyard, growing with many trees that hung over the walls reverently. The paving stones were cracked and weathered through until patches of grass ran wild everywhere.

In the center was a large, blossoming tree, with branches that hung down, never touching the ground. Karen sat under the tree, her arms folded around her knees, her red hair lying motionless on her blue dress.

Wendell stopped for a moment, trying to think of anything to say. She looked up now quickly, and he could see that there were many streaks of tears that had yet to dry. Anger and shame haunted her eyes, but she looked at him boldly, as if to say, "What is it now?"

Then she looked away quickly again, and huddled against the tree. Wendell forced himself to walk forward. If only he could explain, it would all be okay again!!

Karen stared up at him again, as he started to say something. Her words trembled with sadness, but she said them forcefully.

"I know I shouldn't have run away yesterday. But you didn't have to *yell* at me!!"

"...I thought you were Violet!!" he said, hesitantly.

Karen looked up as if she wasn't sure to believe it.

"You have to believe me!" Wendell said.

She looked off to the side, then started saying something, in a little quavery voice.

"I never knew..."

"Never knew what?" he asked quickly.

"...you could be like that!!" she said. "If you could do that to Violet..."

"then what??" Wendell said exasperatedly.

"What about me???" she snapped.

Wendell stood, silenced.

"But you're not Violet!!" he said suddenly. "Who cares about her?"

Karen looked shocked. "She's my sister!!"

"She's always mean to you! But I chose you!! Even though you're not..." he said, bewilderedly.

"...I'm not *pretty* enough? I'm not beautiful like wonderful Violet?!?"

"Look, none of the princes ever chose you! And you weren't even the way I expected!! But I chose you anyways!!"

All along Karen looked like she couldn't think of anything poisonous enough to say. Then suddenly, she got up and ran past Wendell, trying to get away. He tried to follow, but she was gone. "She probably knows a shortcut," he thought vaguely now, as he made his way slowly out from the garden, not even sure it was worth the effort.

48

Garim, the master storyteller, returned to the castle that afternoon and was given lodging by the king. Wendell heard the two of them talking now, in jovial voices, but for some reason he didn't want to be seen.

After looking again and again, he found Karen, sitting in a common room by an empty fireplace. She looked up at him with a semblance of politeness as he entered, her mouth drawn into a line.

Wendell went over and stood by the chair.

"Karen... I..."

She listened, never stirring.

"I love you!!" he said, quietly. "I always did, ever since the painting was..."

"Don't start that again," Karen said brusquely, her voice wincing. "You don't love anyone."

Now she stared back at him fearlessly, as if saying "What do you want?"

He could think of nothing more to say.

Later on that evening, the king threw an enormous banquet, in the great hall where there had been one before. A huge fire burned in the enormous fireplace, and servants went about setting the table with great roasted carcasses and spiced wines and apples, until everything was ready.

Wendell sat in the chair of honor once more, by the king's right hand, and Karen sat at the chair that was empty before, looking down sullenly, never saying anything.

"Is Karen always like this?" Wendell whispered to the king, who was in a jovial mood.

"More or less," he said, sounding truthful.

"She's usually rather quiet. But eat, eat!!" he said, piling a leg of suckling ham on Wendell's plate.

Despite having gone many days without food, Wendell picked at the rich meat. At last, the king stood at his chair, and everyone else followed.

"I would like to welcome again, the master storyteller Garim!"

Everyone gave a hearty cheer and applause, and the old man went over slowly to the chair by the fire and sat down. Then he put back his hood, and looked over at Wendell and nodded in greeting, before looking away at the many faces watching him.

Then he rose from the chair, and threw out his arms dramatically, gesturing.

"I mean now to tell you a story, a story which no one has yet heard, but some have lived."

There was a ripple of murmurs from the crowd.

"It is a story that is true in every word, although some may disbelieve even yet. A story that has not yet ended, but yet seems to have an end. I give you: the legend of Wendell!"

There was a roar of applause and laughter from the table, some indicating that the spiced wine had not been withheld in any measure.

"Behold!! There was once an orphan, who lived on the streets of the royal city. And it came to be that on the eve of his fifteenth birthday, on the moon's tide of Erasth, he received a common dagger for a gift."

"And it so happened that this boy had a friend who was a royal painter, through some dark mixture of fate hidden beyond the eyes of men. And it came to be that he saw a painting, of a girl who smiled so wonderfully, that the sight pierced him through, and he could think of nothing else night and day."

Here Garim stabbed himself with an invisible dagger, and fell on his knees. Karen turned to look at the storyteller, and then shook her hair so that it hung over her face as she looked down.

"And so it came to be, that this girl was a royal princess, and so he despaired of happiness. But one day she was found missing. When the boy heard of it, like a foolish madman he took the shoddy dagger that was his one possession, and demanded entrance to the king from the royal guards, braving perhaps even death or the dungeon."

Here the old man waved about an invisible dagger at hundreds of guards, as if he was insane. The table roared with laughter, and someone patted Wendell heartily on the back.

"And through speaking words of ancient wisdom which have scarce been heard for hundreds of years, he persuaded the king of his mad mission, who sent him with all speed."

"But I forget!!" he said, smacking his forehead. "The girl was said to be lost in a great labyrinth, which all men feared more than death itself. But did this boy wisely consider that, or was he merely heartbroken that he could not find the entrance to this treacherous place?"

"But find it he did. On going through the woods, he saw growing a patch of red flowers, which reminded him of her beautiful hair."

Here Garim tossed his head as if he had long, streaming locks, to the audience's delight.

"And then he saw a bright forest place, which reminded him of her glowing smile."

Here he beamed at everyone, batting his eyes coyly.

"And then, at last, he heard a brook which sounded like her quiet, beautiful voice, even though he had never yet heard it."

And he imitated quite well the murmuring, rushing sounds of water. Karen muttered something poisonous behind her hair.

"Once through, I cannot relate every danger he faced, every obstacle that ensnared the way, for they are far too numerous. The dead returned for vengeance on the living, and his faith and perseverance were put untimely to the test. In riddles was he challenged like no king, and I need not even speak of the black dragons and monstrous creatures which hunted his waking... and sleeping hours."

"But wait!! I forget again!!" he said now, slapping himself on the forehead comically and turning about like a numbskull. "It seems that along the way, he suspected help from a far-off ally, he knew not who. Despite his entreaties, they gave him no sign of prescence, yet through words of yore he knew that they were there."

"And so it came to be that he found the courage to enter that most dreadful of places, the castle... of Aztbane!"

Here some members of the king's court, who had been laughing before, now murmured with disbelief and awe.

"No, my friends, this is no lie. Through the halls of that treacherous place the boy stalked, carrying nothing but his beaten dagger and a bag of stolen jewels. But do you think that he was afraid? Do you think that he huddled in a corner indeed?"

Now Garim made a show of cowering in the chair, his arms drawn up before him like a whipped puppy.

"*No!!* Laughing he went amongst the ghouls, bopping them with diamonds and jewels, sneaking keys from beneath their knees, passing through without a sneeze!!"

The storyteller acted out the words to great effect, and once more laughter filled the halls.

"And so it came that he found the girl, lost and afraid, who had despaired of ever finding her way out."

Here Garim wandered pitifully through a horrid place, until every corner was filled with silence. Karen hung her head behind her hair, though Wendell could not tell what she was thinking.

"And no sooner had he found her, then she was taken again by ogres. But the dear lad followed behind, never knowing it was her, for she had told him a false name."

Now he skulked behind an invisible corner and peered out.

"And when at last he had found her, did he needs face a goblin indeed? An ogre? A foul being? No, I tell you, he found himself face to face with Pale Candle and Hollow Wind, monstrous beings from before the dawn of man, fallen from great heights and ancient in power. Ignorance may suffice for his bravery here."

Garim here drew himself up as if he was a hundred feet tall, and glowered fiercely until Wendell himself wanted to look away.

"Did the fool boy then back off? Did he then admit a mistake? No, for upon seeing the girl asleep there, he threw himself at the immortals, bearing his wretched weapon as if it were lightning."

"With steel against ancient words and strength, the boy dashed them to the ground, and carried away the one his heart knew nothing of."

Garim stumbled silently, carrying something heavy.

"Upon her waking, there was no time but for flight, and so they made their way down to the dungeons of that evil place, and to the lair where was kept an astounding creature... the Wyvern!! Thereupon he loosed the monster from its bonds, and holding on to the chain, both of them were pulled out from the walls of the castle and flown across the hidden labyrinth to the very entrance he had come in through at first."

"Cleansed with wind and water, the girl's face shone for all to see now, and he recognized her at last. And so it was that they made their way back to the castle, and were sworn to be reunited forever."

Everyone began clapping and cheering now, pleasantly, but Garim raised a hand, and the noise died down.

"But what can I say of the one who aided the boy? The one he called upon in his darkest moments, and who led him through ways unknown? What can be said of them?"

After a few terse moments, Garim sat in his chair, and it became apparent that the story was ended. Now everyone clapped again, but more sparsely this time.

For the rest of the feast, Wendell sat in silence.

49

The next day, Wendell found himself out in the gardens again. The quiet beauty around him seemed to give calmer answers to his questions than his own turmoiled thoughts did. The sun was so warm, but still it never soaked into the coldness inside. When he did see Karen in the sitting room sometimes, she was polite and talked with him if he said anything, but always there was something missing from her voice that he wished for now, different than when she had been Kimberly. So he went about the castle and the gardens, because there was nothing else to do.

It isn't right! He thought dismally. She was only a few feet away, but he couldn't find her anymore, not like when she was a hundred miles away in Aztbane.

"Just because I was mean to Violet, doesn't mean I would be mean to her!" Wendell thought, but as hard as he tried, he couldn't find a way to prove that it wasn't true. But it must not be!!

Eventually, he found a place under the castle, full of old books and scrolls, some hundreds of years old, and the guard quickly moved aside to allow him in. The darkness of the place seemed to match Wendell's brooding mood, and he spent many hours looking through pages, trying to find something to think about.

"Vanity of vanities, says the Teacher, all things are vanity!! Go, live your vain life, with the wife whom you love, and eat your food with gladness, but know that this too is vanity, and a chasing after the wind..."

Wendell shuddered and opened a different book.

"Faithful are the wounds from a friend, but an enemy multiplies kisses..."

What is that supposed to mean?

"...Their words are smoother than oil, but they are drawn swords..."

Will no one say anything helpful?

"If anyone hates another, they are a murderer!"

How depressing!!

Most puzzling of all were Garim's final words the night before. What had happened to the one who helped him? Perhaps it was the fairy queen! But she had told him he was perfect, and then a voice said he wasn't. Perhaps they were lying.

But wasn't that the same voice that helped him defeat the two men, and told him not to take the blue stone? And didn't the two men also say he was perfect, just like the queen had? Perhaps they were pretending to lie, to trick him, and... it all didn't make any sense at all! If they were truly his friend, what could they even do now?

Wendell tried calling out for them again, but no one responded, no whisper came, and so he found himself going back down the castle halls again, his mood foul. Maybe they were playing a game. Maybe his life was a giant joke to them, and they were having some fun... they had no reason, no right to let his life fall apart now, to raise up his hopes and then...

"Sir..." he heard a servant say.

Wendell suddenly seized the terrified servant and threw him against a wall with great force.

"Can't you see I'm trying to think!?" Wendell screamed in his face, then let him go, suddenly. The servant ran off, never looking back. Wendell looked at his hands with sadness and kept going down the empty hall.

50

"I don't understand," Wendell said darkly to Garim, as they walked together by the garden's gate.

"You have said those words before," the storyteller said, grimly.

"Yes, but... now I really mean them. Now I don't even know what I'm supposed to not be understanding. Nothing makes sense anymore. I don't understand my life."

"Perhaps that is a good thing," Garim said, opaquely. "Those who claim to understand their life are usually fools or gods."

Wendell felt a growing frustration as he talked with the old man. Garim was his friend, he always had been, he knew, even though at times he seemed deliberately difficult. But now, when Wendell needed him most, he couldn't even begin to explain his nameless thoughts to the old man.

"Before I left the castle... I had a dream," Wendell confided.

Garim said nothing.

"Someone... told me, that I was... the perfect one. That, stars sang when I was born!"

Garim looked off into the distance.

"Do you believe it?" he said seriously.

Wendell wanted to answer yes, but he could think of no reason, no explanation to back it up, to explain how he had felt in the dream!

"I see," the old storyteller mulled.

"And what would Karen say about it?" he said suddenly.

Wendell didn't know what he was getting at, but he could see Karen's face clearly, telling him that he wasn't so perfect, indeed!!

Wendell said nothing, and soon they parted ways, with no more words to say, and he was left alone again with himself, to argue endlessly about what the old man had said, even though he didn't understand a word of it. If he didn't understand, why did it bother him so much?

51

Over the next days, before the wedding was planned to begin, Wendell's mood was strange and surreal. He sat in his room, looking at one of the open chests of gold coins. He let the coins fall through his fingers again and again, wishing that somehow they were not so hard and cold.

The scroll room yielded only more horrible sayings, and he found the garden's bright spaces to be the only respite from the wretched chill that hung over him always and seeped even into his bones.

Soon it was only a day from the wedding, at the end of the preparation week. There was another great banquet that night, to celebrate the wedding. Garim sat by the fire during the whole night, never stirring or saying anything. Finally, at the end of the banquet, he turned in the chair, and put back his hood slowly.

"Of all the stories that have been told, this is the greatest," he began in a low, brooding voice.

"Of all the legends that are known, this one is the truest," he continued...

"Of all the trials that have been faced, this one was the most terrible."

Then he paused for a long time, until everyone became uneasy.

"*Behold!!*" he roared at last, never stirring in the chair.

"It came to be that Ren Zael, the great warrior, was born into the earth to hear the cries of the lost and the wails of the forgotten. To seek the one he loved, he came, though she was dead already, and her beauty had left her."

No one in the room stirred.

"And great was the light of his face upon the children of men, so that even the darkness of night fled from his presence, and the bonds of all who sought his aid were loosed."

Now his voice lowered to a growl.

"But there were those who did not wish it so. And so they trapped him, and put him to death by torturous means, and he did not resist them."

A child at the far end of the table gasped.

"And so to the bottom of the worlds he went, where the great serpent, the Dragon, awaited to devour him forever, who had sought his life."

"Many days they fought, down in that hideous realm, where none can leave, and hope is not remembered for days and ages to come. I cannot tell of the grievous blows and forgotten mysteries by which they fought, but know only this: that in the end Ren Zael was victorious, and rose again to life."

"Many say it is only a lie. Many say it is but a story. For where is Ren Zael now, if indeed he came to life again? To what end of the world shall we go to seek him, to what heights must we rise to find him, whom not even death could destroy?"

"But it is rumored that someday he will return to the affairs of men. But watch carefully for the day of his coming, for it is like a thief coming at night."

The fire had grown down to a smoldering crackle. With this, Garim turned and looked directly in Wendell's eyes, his voice lowered to an urgent whisper.

"For the coming of destiny... is like the coming of death... swift, unexpected, and final."

With that, the old man turned away and looked into the fire, never stirring.

52

Wendell wandered aimlessly through the castle's many corridors at midnight, unable to find any sleep in his room.

"I wish I could do it all over again," he thought, to no one, not even himself. "If only they sent me out again, I could fight just as well as I did before!! I'm the one who did everything," he thought bitterly. "I'm the one who was brave and did what everyone else was too cowardly for!! I'm the one who risked my life again and again, for this sad ungrateful girl nobody likes!"

Where was the nameless one that supposedly helped him? If they were so great, why couldn't they help him now?

"I'm the one who did it all. I'm the one who had to be great and clever and all, just like Curdie and David always were! I didn't need any help anyways! Why would I??" he thought, on and on.

Finally, he found himself at the doorway of a small, round room. Someone was standing on a small pedestal with her back to Wendell, her arms stretched out for the royal measurers, bright red hair flowing down the white gown she was wearing.

Now they turned her around, and she looked back at Wendell as if to say, "Are you happy now?", still holding out her arms as the servants bustled and measured her.

Wendell went through the halls at random now, his thoughts too horrible for words. One after the other, the passages fled before him, as he tried to find something, he didn't know what.

A servant came running into view, a fearful look on his face.

"The king requests your presence in the royal chambers," he said, panting. "Violet is gone!"

Wendell was led in a stupor to the throne room. The king stood, below his throne, some weary looking military commanders gathered about him. When he saw Wendell, he rushed over to him, his face empty and anguished.

"My dear boy, if anyone can help me, you can!!" The king said, his voice sadly eager.

"You must be off at once in pursuit!! I have arranged for horses. I am sorry, but you must be off before the kidnappers have gotten too far!! If anyone can help... if anyone..."

With that, Wendell was led with the commanders, Hangs leading them diligently, out to the royal stables, where several pages were busy dressing up warhorses and stallions.

Now Wendell mounted his old horse, and the others did the same. Together, they cantered about towards the castle bridge. The sky was cloudy and dark, and soon, droplets of moisture were falling.

As they reached the bridge, Wendell heard someone cry out behind him.

"Wendell!!"

He looked behind as the horses sped ahead, and saw Karen running after him in the rain, her wedding dress soaked with water. She tripped now, and caught herself, and looked up again. He always remembered the way her face looked, the rain streaking her hair into dark rivulets across her face, looking so sad, so sad...

53

They galloped and cantered on into the early morning, never stopping to rest, and Wendell could hear Hangs conferring darkly with the other commanders as they went.

Wendell's mood was dismal as the sun began rising up on the horizon. He itched in all the worst places, and the saddle seemed to dig into his skin whenever the horse turned. He slunk in his saddle, wanting to holler with annoyance, but he couldn't. He was desperately tired, not even having gotten any sleep at all the previous night. But the road continued blearily for a long time, until he was ready to tip out of the saddle.

Soon they had reached the branch in the path, where they had gone before. He looked up at the dark sky above to the left, where the Lonely Wilds was. The Aelahna pass lay below, and he looked down at it longingly. But they were not going there this time. Before, when he had gone past the Lonely Wilds, he had briefly imagined how it would be and then forgotten it, but now he felt the long-forgotten feelings of fear and dread sneaking in.

They climbed up the rocky path, the horses' large hoofs clambering and stomping quickly over the rocks, and Wendell clung to his horse, feeling weary. Questions went around inside without any words, never getting anywhere.

At least before he had faced death willingly, but he didn't even care whether Violet lived or died. She had ruined everything.

A horrible, seething feeling went through him as he heard her taunting voice again, then saw Karen's humiliated eyes as she dropped the flowers.

Soon, after an eternity of bumpy misery, the path leveled out a bit and the land steepened on either side into crumbly slopes that looked as if they could collapse at any moment. The men went through them silently, looking up watchfully at either side.

Wendell noticed that some of them kept one hand rested on their sword hilt. In the distance now and then, black shapes flew through the sliver of sky, but it was hard to see how large they were.

Hangs stopped at the head of the train, looking up at the sky. His great horse stirred a bit, but he calmed it harshly. Wendell heard something like the memory of a bad, distant dream, a rising wail. It turned into a fierce screech, and a shadow flashed over them. Hangs turned his horse about, the hooves kicking up into the air, and shouted to the men to watch the sky.

The horses were pressed along more quickly now, almost galloping through the treacherous piles of rock, their mouths spitting foam. Now Wendell's horse reared up, and he almost fell onto the sharp ground.

Hangs yelled something and drew his sword, and Wendell heard men doing the same behind him. He clung to the horse's neck as it swerved about.

A bloodthirsty cry deafened Wendell's ears, making him scream with pain, as blackness descended over them. The twang of many arrows sliced the air faintly, and the wail rose with fervent, hawkish rage.

Then he was on the ground, looking up at the sky. For one moment a huge eye stared down at him, merciless. Then the beak turned and snapped at a rider, knocking them off their mount. There were cries of fear and war.

The hawk rose up, talons bared at Wendell as he tried to turn over, but somehow couldn't. Hangs struck with his broadsword, slicing through feathers, and someone dragged Wendell up and away.

54

He woke up, and everything was still. Wendell sat up a bit, clutching at his side. It was wrapped with wet cloth. Then a dizziness overtook him and he flopped down again. When he opened his eyes, Hangs and another looked down at him. He heard the general's gruff voice.

"He'll be okay in a few days. At least he didn't break any bones. From now on we'll send a scouting party ahead, even if it means less protection at the rear guard."

For the next days or nights, Wendell had a consciousness of being carried along on something. Slowly he became more conscious, and finally was able to sit on his horse again, although going more slowly than before.

At last the pass widened out up ahead, and Hangs brought the line to a standstill. The scouting party came hurrying back, and when they reached the main group, Wendell could see a look of fear. Hangs motioned for Wendell to follow him, and they went up alone, until he could see a flat valley ahead, full of dark twisted rocks.

"I always hate to lose a good fighter," Hangs said, sounding almost wistful. "If it were up to me, I'd train you for a general and forget about the king's spoiled kid."

He put out his hand for Wendell to shake, who didn't take it.

"I'm honored to have known you. If you come back without Violet though, the king will have your head."

With that, Hangs turned and led his horse back down. Wendell got off the horse awkwardly, and it suddenly turned and whinnied, going back as well.

"You can't just leave me here!!" Wendell shouted at Hangs. There was no reply.

Wendell watched as the line of men slowly disappeared. His eyes watered with the dust and stale air. Then he turned and looked across the valley; it didn't seem to have any sense to it. Rocks rose up and sank down in ludicrous ways, making hideous, stark forms. There were black shapes flying below the dark clouds always, and sometimes he thought he could hear the cry of falcons, far up.

"If I was Curdie," he thought desperately, "I would know what to do!! I would be able to find Violet, just like in every good story... and then go back to Karen!!... Curdie was good and true, and unselfish and resourceful and..."

The hawks would see him soon! He had to get under some of those rocks, fast!!

Looking up fearfully, Wendell, hurried out of the pass and into the valley. Hopefully nothing had seen him yet. What was he doing here? After climbing over a messy pile of slippery stones, he found refuge under a small hanging outcropping.

What am I doing here? he thought, hugging himself and looking out through the opening. How did I end up in a place like this?? Wendell thought back over his life, and there seemed to be no reason, no point to it! He couldn't stay in here forever!

Or maybe he could. If only... if only... what? But wishing endlessly didn't make anything change.

Karen had come running after him, at least!! But if he went back, they would kill him! He stifled a scream of rage, but it didn't die, it just boiled inside.

Maybe... he could sneak back and find her and run away and... or if he did find Violet... that horrid girl who didn't deserve to live... who tricked him... who should die...

A hundred times he made up his mind to leave the cave, but never did. He heard the cries of huge ravens and crows, and saw strange creatures spindling across the ground far away.

Now there was a strange wail, different than a bird. It was a lost, pleading sound that terrified him, he didn't know why, and he crawled to the edge of the opening and looked out. There was something going along quickly, something humanish, with long dark hair. Another wail came from it, and he went to the edge of the opening now.

"Wendell!! Is that you?" he heard Violet's voice, trembling and tearful. It was Violet! Wendell started climbing out of the crevice.

"They're coming!!" she shouted. Wendell heard the nightmarish shriek of birds again, and froze with fear. He forced himself out of the opening, though, and then looked up at the sky. Two ravens, larger than he believed possible, were soaring down to the ground, their claws outstretched. Violet saw his face and looked behind.

He thought for a long moment of what he should... what should he do?? The raven wrapped its talons around Violet and picked her up into the sky. He shrunk against the rock and heard her scream fade into the distance. The other raven flew about, watching. There was no time but to scramble back into the cavern and try to hide.

Wendell sat miserably against the stone. He noticed that his hands were shaking violently. What had he done?? He had failed! Now he would never see Karen again!! If only he hadn't been so angry and hateful, maybe Violet would... but it was *her fault! She deserved this!*

His face twisted between sadness and rage. Wendell looked at the huge, endless black sky above him. He was just an orphan on the streets again, not like Curdie's stories at all, alone and hopeless.

Who cared about Violet. She didn't really matter! *What could he have done anyways?* His only hope now was if they were taking her somewhere not too far away, but what hope was that...

Now he fought to drag himself out of the cave again, grimacing against all the terror in every direction. He wasn't going to die like a fool! It wasn't going to be this way!

Quickly Wendell shamed himself for looking for another cave to run to. But it would be so pointless to stay in the open!! Wendell went along now, climbing over rocks and pits hurriedly. A cry of hunger filled his ears again, and he quickly found refuge under a rock again as a shadow crossed the land.

He crossed from one hiding place to another, always heading towards where the raven had flown, feeling a momentary security before forcing himself out into the open again.

Misery pressed him forward, as if he was trying to get away from something, but never quite made it. One time a band of black, spindly creatures surrounded him, coming from all sides, and he struck and spun about with terrible force, spitting curses at them and splitting them open on every side, bashing their forms without mercy or thought, letting out all the hatred and despair.

He kicked the dead bodies aside violently now, and wiped off a grimy tear from his weeping face, before ducking below a tilted stone. There was something terrible happening inside him, and he muttered to himself with black words. If he ever made it back alive, he would show them their mistake! He could see himself throwing the king off of his throne... servants ran from him as he cut them down without mercy...

He almost felt himself smile at the terrible visions of ruin and destruction. Who needed Violet anyways? He had made it through those horrid mazes! He could go back and sneak into the castle again and who would stop him?! He was the perfect one! And Karen would rule beside him!!

But he thought of Karen's face if he came back without Violet, screaming at him...

Soon thirst was beginning to come, but Wendell pressed himself onward mercilessly over a black, deformed hill. He would succeed, just like Curdie had in every story! Surely, he was a true hero like Curdie had been, he must be! After all, he had been one before! He was so great and noble at heart, as his own father must have been once! The stars all sang about him when he was born, and he was the...

"Your father is the Dragon."

Wendell stopped, completely astonished.

It was the same whisper as before, calmly spoken. Once again he felt with a pang as if he knew who was speaking to him, the one who had guided him all along. But that couldn't be true. Enemies must be taunting him, trying to discourage him! But they weren't going to stop him! What a filthy lie.

What infuriated him most was that the words were so calm and so gentle. If the whisper had been harsh and vengeful, full of savage fury, it would be so easy to push it away... but he knew he should ignore it.

Wendell's mood was foul now. He clambered over another ridge, cursing as he cut his hand on a sharp edge, looking up fearfully at the black shapes. The whispered words had filled him with an empty feeling of dread. His father was a dragon? But dragons were spiteful, and proud and full of vengeance...

"Your father... was the Dragon."

The words came again. He shoved them away. No one could help him if that was true! They had all left him to die!

"You're all demons!" Wendell roared at nobody and nothing, covering his face against the stale wind. Several black shapes swerved and came towards him, and he gasped and jumped into an empty hole without looking, scurrying into a dark corner, pleading with no one and covering his ears against the blind shrieks of the hawks and crows and ravens.

Filthy tears ran down his face now, and he tried to huddle somewhere inside and find comfort, but found only fear and anger and despair instead.

Why did they all leave him to die? Why help him all along, just to end it now? Wendell muttered horrible things, but it only made him feel sadder.

A huge beak poked into the hole, and Wendell stabbed at it furiously, slashing at its most vulnerable places and roaring threats at it. Finally the bird retreated in pain, and Wendell heard the scuttling of legs coming near... soon they would be there, no telling how many!

If he ever made it back alive, the king would have to answer for leaving him here to die! Wendell gritted his teeth and saw a vision of the king's face as he fell off the throne, gasping for life under the dagger's blade. Guards would come forward, but Wendell had tricked them all before. He could sneak around and take them all, one by one if needed! He didn't march through the fortress of Aztbane just to be left here by some cowardly kingdom, full of ignorant fools that deserve to suffer...

Far away he could see the clouds open up. Wendell saw a single star shining, with a beautiful song of love and hope. But now he covered his eyes against the joyful song, he needed to shout it out as it mocked him.

"Where are you all?" Wendell snipped at the air.

He looked up unseeingly at the star again, and clouds started to move back. Surely they could help him, but if he really was a dragon's son, if he was turning into his father, why would they even want to?

He searched desperately for any story he had heard... always the treacherous ones died and only the good lived. But who even cared?? Stupid stories didn't keep him alive now! *He would write his own story, with their blood! A story greater than...*

He could feel the rage and despair coming again and didn't know who he was anymore. There was nowhere to go to escape what was happening.

In a fit of sudden terror, Wendell screamed through the darkness.

"Great warrior Ren Zael! Please help me!"

No answer. Then, so quietly he could hardly hear it, he heard the whisper...

"With what?"

Wendell turned his head away from the stars, and closed his eyes tightly.

"A dragon's heart," he said.

But nothing happened. A small, warm breeze kicked about in the hole. Wendell thought back now to the stories again, to Curdie and David, so brave and great. It felt as if he could remember them so clearly, as if they were here with him now... then it seemed as if someone was there, close somewhere. The feeling became stronger, grew ancient and more majestic, until it was all around.

Wendell opened his eyes, and the feeling grew more and more until it burst open around him brightly, until he could see it, glistening with the morning sun, singing with a voice as pure as gold, a song so joyful that tears came to his eyes until he could hardly bear it.

The light never blinded him, it seemed as if it had been there all along, even in the miserable hole, only he had never noticed it before.

It was a very different kind of light than the fairy queen's had been, that had seemed to whisper all the wonderful things that he could ever want to hear, but this light made him tremble and weep and laugh and smile all at the same time, and he wished it would never go away.

Out of the light he saw a face now, and hands, and feet, that seemed to have horrible gashes and wounds on them. He trembled inside when he saw the man's face now, so kind it was behind the scars, looking at Wendell with a noble and gentle look.

Wendell opened his mouth to say something, but even though he had a hundred things to say, he couldn't find a way to say any of them. Now the man spoke, in the voice he had heard whispering so many times before. Wendell realized how majestic it was, and wondered why he hadn't noticed that before.

55

"Yes, I am Ren Zael, the one you have known in stories. Long ago I came to the world and I defeated the great Dragon which preys on all men."

Finally Wendell managed to say something.

"But why did you leave? Why can't anyone find you when you are needed?"

He looked at Wendell with understanding.

"I left my spirit here! And so I could be wherever someone needed me, anywhere they were. But this knowledge of my presence was lost over the years, and since no one could feel or hear me anymore... I became a legend. A story. Now I am nothing but a myth."

"Only if someone called on me, truly knowing that I was there, could I help them and re-enter the land! I have searched for many years, all across the kingdom for someone who might do it, but found none. For too long the Dragon has found a hiding place, hiding deep within the hearts of all men and women, wearing many masks, but now you have found me! The one who defeated him."

"*I was the one who listened* when you asked if the stories were true. *I was the one who watched you* as you heard the minstrel's songs and looked at the empty sky."

"*I was the one who heard you* in the wheat field, wishing for things long gone."

"*I was the one who answered you* when you needed to pass the guards, because I thought you might someday call upon me."

"*I was the one who told you the Truth*, that you are not perfect, when that foul mistress Danala came with her beauteous, flattering words and heart of pride."

"*I was the one who left clues* for you to enter the labyrinth, and sent a wolf to show you the way, although I could do no more until you allowed it."

"*I was the one who carried you* through the fortress of Aztbane and defeated the two fallen angels, for my own sake. I told you not to listen or take that stone, or all would be undone."

"*I was the one who hoped* that you would remember me, and call upon me, but you became proud at heart and believed the lie."

"*I was the one who told you* that your father was the Dragon."

"And I am the one who has snatched you from his power now. Just as you gave much for Karen, so I gave everything to rescue you all, even my life.

"*I was the one who made you love her*, and it was my own love for all the forsaken that you felt. Tell her that I have been listening. And I am *not* imaginary."

"You have been through much, but now that you have found me, do not keep these things a secret as others have in the past, or I will be forgotten again!!"

"You must remember that I will be with you, I will be *in* you, forever. I will speak to you in a new way. Go now. See that Violet is held in a cave to the north. You must forgive her, and yourself, or I can do nothing at all."

He smiled brightly, like the dawn of purest morning.

"Don't fear anymore, Wendell. All of your great dreams will be true after all…"

Wendell nodded gravely, and then the brightness vanished.

56

Wendell sat there in the miserable hole. Somehow he felt peaceful now, even if his whole body still ached, but he noticed that the thirst had gone.

He looked up out at the sky, and saw the stars shining again. Singing brightly, shining brightly, of love and courage and hope. Violet was still alive!

He felt an old feeling of hatred rise up, and words of anger. But he pushed it all aside. Now he climbed up out of the hole, and looked to the north, where Ren Zael had pointed... there was indeed an opening there, in the base of a weird hill.

Wendell scurried furiously from one place to another, trying to reach the entrance without being seen. At last he reached it and huddled there. Waves of simmering, fiery heat flowed out every now and then, and a seething glow of red light flickered inside.

He stepped through, and stopped. The inside of the entire hill was vacant and glowed with an ember's dark heat. There were mounds of golden treasures and diamonds, heaped up like mountains of mere dust and scattered everywhere.

An enormous dragon statue made of red jewels lounged on top of it all, smoldering like living coals. The statue had a long, serpentine body, with huge curving claws tucked under its wise, pointed face.

Two jaded, inscrutable eyes stared at Wendell as if they didn't even care that he was there, over a mouth that curved with many beautiful fangs, wrapped in a smirk of eternal coyness. The statue blinked.

Wendell heard something speak in his mind, as he tried to tear his eyes away from the statue's mysterious gaze.

"I suppose... you're looking... for them."

Wendell didn't reply.

"I suppose you think... I'm like the black dragon."

He heard something like a giggle.

"Damarisk is a fool... who sleeps too... too much. I... haven't slept... in... five... thousand years."

Wendell slowly reached for the dagger's hilt.

"Don't worry... about using.... that, Wendell."

Another giggle.

"I know about Pale... Candle... and Hollow Wind. No concern... I'm much... older... than them... you know."

"You humans... don't... know... our… power over you..."

Wendell spoke up rashly at last.

"You don't have any power over me, you old liar!!"

The great statue blinked again, and smiled wider and wider. The air quaked for a moment but then stopped.

"You don't even... know... that you already belong... to... us... the… dra... gons... and you..."

"That story has ended, Nemurthis." Wendell heard himself say, not even knowing what he was saying or why. "Ren Zael has returned to the realm of men. This child is beyond your reach now!"

The eyes blinked again, leisurely, and a billow of steam came from between the fangs. It felt like there was an earthquake, but nothing was moving. Then all was silence again, like a forgotten tomb.

"Ren Zael is... a... silly... dream of the... children... he cannot help... you..."

"I know that you are lying!" Wendell said through his teeth, drawing the dagger swiftly, although his hand trembled as he held on to it tightly.

"Then you... will carry it all to... the underworld... where no... one can... ever hear... you... again..." went the smiling voice, hollow as a graveyard bell.

57

The huge statue towered up with a rush of strength and fury and lunged for him. Wendell threw the dagger as hard as he could, as the giant jaws opened around him. It plunged between the open teeth, and Wendell was thrown backwards onto the ground as the mouth snapped shut with a grimace of agony.

The huge body thrashed and rolled around in a horrible way, the claws grasping for the buried blade. Golden treasures scattered like pebbles as the dragon roared and scratched with its powerful talons in a terrible dance of pain and despair.

Quickly Wendell rolled over, and found a large gold-encrusted broadsword.

Inside he heard terrible shrieks from the dragon's voice, cursing him in a hundred languages at once. Dragging the massive sword behind, he saw the statue grow stiff for a moment, claws pawing at the air, although smoke still boiled out of the mouth. He aimed carefully between two red jewels where the heart might be. With a tremendous, horrible heave, he swung the heavy broadsword over his head, and pushing with all his meager weight now, the huge blade sliced through, sending it deep into the dragon's body, which quivered horribly now and then lay still.

Exhausted with the effort, Wendell collapsed on the ground and tried to catch his breath.

There was a noise from something else. He staggered up quickly.

Violet came stumbling out from behind the piles of gold, looking shaken and amazed. She looked at the silent, sprawled corpse and then back at Wendell, as if she didn't know what was going on, tears of terror still in her eyes.

"It wasn't me," Wendell said weakly. "I saw Ren Zael, and he told me, a lot of things," he said, trying to explain.

Violet just kept looking at him as if he was some kind of ghastly being, still unable to say anything at all.

58

Princess Karen sat by the window and looked out at the gardens. It had been days since Wendell left. She had tried to convince herself that she hated him so much and was glad he was finally dead, but now it was too late for her to change her mind!

She tried going out to her special tree and talking with her imaginary friend. Somehow it wasn't the same anymore. She heard about the ancient warrior Ren Zael in the children's stories, and ever since had imagined that he was her only special friend, and told him about everything, but at the end she knew it was just a sad game. Even if she wished it wasn't, more than anything else.

Slowly, she got up and walked, out to the gardens, to her special tree again. Maybe this time...

"Hello," she said, looking up as if he had just come into the courtyard.

"What took you so long," she said, smiling tearfully.

His kind, wise eyes looked back at her, in her game.

"I had to chase another ogre away," he said. "It was stealing turnips from the farmers."

She tossed her hair to one side as if pouting.

"Well maybe next time you should do it much more quickly! I was getting concerned."

He laughed kindly. Then he said... he said... it was...

"Oh, what would he say next?" Karen said miserably. The game usually lasted way longer than this! Karen sat down under the tree and wrapped her arms around her knees. She looked up at the white flowers, that hung like beautiful bells. Everything felt so empty now. Before Wendell had come, she was always happy! At least while in her own secret place, away from everyone else. Why did he have to show up.

Now she woke up, and realized it was getting dark already. She must have fallen asleep for a long time! Not wanting anyone to notice, Karen crept back into the castle, and tiptoed down a hall. She stopped. A servant stood waiting. He looked so worried.

"Your father sent me to tell you that Wendell has returned... but I couldn't find you..."

Without hearing another word, she turned and ran down the hall, but then slowed to a walk. Would he even want to see her anymore? Or was he changed into a miserable, beastly person now, even more angry than he always seemed to be before...

There was a fire in Wendell's room, and the door was open, but she couldn't see anyone in there! Creeping in, she looked all around. There was a chair next to the hearth, and she came and looked, carefully.

Wendell sat in the chair, wrapped in a blanket, looking pale. He looked up at her wearily, and something was different about him, but not in a bad way. Before he always seemed to have a sour look in his face somewhere, even while smiling. But now he was more quiet than before.

She looked back at him, not knowing what she could say.

Finally Wendell was trying to say something.

"I saw him."

What was he talking about??

"Who?" she said quickly.

"Ren Zael."

Karen felt as if she was afraid, but for no reason.

"It's true! How else could I still be alive?! I only asked him to help me. To keep me from having... a Dragon's heart. And then, he was there!"

"He told me a lot of things, I don't remember them all. I can't possibly tell you what it was like! He even talked about you."

"He also told me, I should tell you that he was listening. I don't know why!"

It might have been a trick if it was someone else! But Wendell was so serious, as he always had been! Maybe he knew something more, could tell her something else...

"Could you ask him to appear again?"

Wendell shook his head sadly. No one said anything for a while. Then Karen had to ask something.

"What do you mean a dragon's heart?! Is that something else he said? Did he say anything else?"

Karen could hardly believe her own words, that she was asking someone who had seen her ancient warrior. It had been a stupid game for so long, but know she didn't know anything anymore! She wanted to ask a hundred things right away, but couldn't think of anything else to say. She wanted Wendell to just answer right now, but then for some reason she felt like she couldn't bear to hear a single word. Everything was different and impossible and terrifying because it couldn't be true but it had to be true!

Wendell gave a sad little laugh. Then he looked away at a corner with painful eyes for a while.

"Do I really need to tell you? You saw me before. I was so filled up with my own sorrow. In a way, all the things I did were just really for myself. But I didn't even know anything until I was about to die!"

Then Violet's haughty voice sounded from the doorway.

"So, you're telling her new lies now?" she said, in her proud, regal voice. But there was so much sorrow in it now, that it was strange to hear.

She looked much different than Karen had ever seen her, as if a golden mask had fallen off, leaving someone smaller behind. Violet kept on talking though, as if it wasn't possible to stop.

"I knew I was dead... I promised a thousand times I would do anything if I could just go home... the dragon just laughed at me... I felt so alone, and so small, but the dragon asked me how many times I had laughed at someone's despair... but I just wanted to go home..."

Finally her voice stopped, as if she was a servant girl who had been caught in the wrong room, and looked at her hands. Wendell remembered something, and looked up eagerly.

"I remember Ren Zael said anyone could find him again. If they only they knew that he was there they could find him," Wendell said hopefully. "That's how..."

Violet spoke up impulsively.

"Ren Zael! If you..."

Then suddenly Violet stopped and looked up, a surprised and happier look on her face than before.

Then Karen said something, quickly.

"Do you still remember me? Karen?"

Wendell found himself speaking up for some reason, his words changing somehow to a long lost song that he had never even heard before, but that he did know, in a way he didn't understand.

"Great warrior, come free our hearts...."

"...from the dragon's deep dark stain.

From the lies that hide our pride,

make us pure and true again!"

And the others joined in, not knowing how they knew the words.

"Pure as we were meant to be,

true at heart, so brave and free,

heal our story's destiny,

from our desolate wandering!"

"Ren Zael, come free us all,

from the pain of dark within,

take away the old and bring,

new eyes to begin again."

Then, not knowing why, they looked at each other, and Wendell felt as if Ren Zael was there with him again. They all knew. They knew the secret, that he was here, that he was there, that he was with them, now, and always would be.

59

The three of them sat under a garden tree on a bright day, and it seemed like there wasn't much to do.

Wendell looked over. It seemed so strange to be friends with Violet now, as if nothing had ever happened. It was like all the horrible things they had said were not even a dream. But the strange ancient secrets they shared now had brought them all together, as if they had known each other forever.

"We have to tell someone that the old songs were true," Wendell said. "Your father would want us to tell him something so important!"

Karen suddenly looked up at him, twisting some grass blades together in her hands anxiously.

"Who's even going to believe that? Some children with a crazy story like that?"

"Ren Zael told me not to keep anything a secret. He said it was very important! Otherwise everything will be forgotten again! That's what matters!"

Violet smiled a little.

"Maybe we should go tell that crazy storyteller! He's always talking about crazy, impossible things."

"He's not really crazy!" Wendell said. "Well, not that much, anyways."

Then they laughed, and felt that things might be more serious, and more fun, and more important, and more mysterious than all the wishes they had used to hope for before.

Epilogue

Over the next days, preparations for the wedding were renewed. Old, withering garlands that had faded since the day Wendell left were replaced, and new meats were prepared and stuffed, and spiced wines were re-poured.

The servants were very busy, and the king spared no expense. But there was much muttering among the servants about the strange happenings of the past days.

Wendell and Karen sat now under the tree of blooms, far from the ears of the serving maids. Karen rested her head on his shoulder, and said something quietly.

"Even though I knew everything could never be real, I still wished for it to be true and waited for it, because it was the only thing I had left."

Then Wendell said something as well.

"Even though I knew I could never find you, that it was stupid to even try, I still searched so much because it was the only thing I had left as well."

www.ingramcontent.com/pod-product-compliance
Lightning Source LLC
Chambersburg PA
CBHW030239030726
47493CB00023B/259